The Hangman Mystery

John Tallon Jones

Published by G-L-R (Great Little Reads)

CONTENTS

Winter 1987

CHAPTER ONE

The old lady is dressed in a cheap black ripped tweed overcoat with thick support stockings and flat shoes. She wears a scruffy old grey corduroy baseball cap pulled down over her eyes, which looks a bit out of place, but serves its purpose of protecting her head from the bitterly cold wind that is blowing on Stanley Street.

She is carrying a large canvas holdall, which slows her down a bit, as she painfully shuffles her way towards the junction with Wickerman Terrace. Here, she has the choice of going left towards the town centre, or right for the Easterman Estate and the sheltered accommodation in Park Gardens. The fact that she turns and trundles back down the road she has just walked up is surprising but not half as strange as the fact that she stops at the junction with Haswell Avenue, turns around and repeats her laboured journey for the second time.

It is ten thirty on a damp Monday evening in Croxley. At a quarter to twelve, she is still out there shuffling and has completed the trip for at least the twentieth time.

The boys swagger aggressively down Stanley Street chanting and playfully jockeying each other. They are wearing their stolen

European designer clothes and shouting at the top of their voices in exaggerated heavy Scouse.

"Liverpool, Liverpool, Liverpool."

"Come on Yooooo Reds."

They're all 'well hard' in their own heads, with the collective mentality of mixed infants. They're a team of scallies after a night in the boozer, with barely a brain cell between the lot of them and a belly full of pent up fury. There are four in the crew; all thinking the same, all talking the same and all dressed the same. They are proudly wearing their Peter Storm Jackets, straight leg jeans and Adidas trainers. These lads carry an attitude against the world with pride and are all tanked up on watered down beer, speed, dope and tribal gang supremacy.

"We hate Everton, and we hate Everton."

"We are the Everton haters."

The youngest is no more than sixteen and the oldest closing in on twenty and a life of dole and individual obscurity. They're on the lookout for easy trouble tonight, and when they set eyes on the old lady clutching her ragged old bag, they think it's their birthday and Christmas all rolled into one. They nudge each other, and the singing stops. It's game on lads with only them as winners, or so it seems.

What they don't know just yet, is that the little old lady feels the same after setting eyes on them.

CHAPTER TWO

Surveillance never was a job that I enjoyed that much. I'd been looking up at the bedroom window of number 29 Stanley Street for about three hours. I was suffering from severe neck cramp and boredom. I'd followed Councillor Evans here from his cosy detached family home out in Speke, and been waiting outside ever since. The window was above a rundown newsagent shop that was partially boarded up, and the woman who had let Evans in didn't look as if she was his sister.

I poured myself a cup of hot tomato soup, from my thermos, and settled down with a copy of the Daily Mirror. I had already read it once and was now tackling the horoscopes in desperation. Mine said that I was about to go on a long journey, the lucky number for Sagittarians was three and red would play a significant part in my day.

My highly strung and very posh girlfriend, Cynthia, had flown off in a huff to the Caribbean, with her equally posh friends, having failed to persuade me that it would be a good idea to escape the weather. To be frank, I prefer the freezing cold and damp to the people she hangs around with so I have only got myself to blame. Sitting in some beach bar in Antigua, drinking rum and coke with Lady C, and having to watch one of her mates being debagged by the Eton/ Oxford set would have been something that would have driven me nuts. Call me plain old working class, but I find no interest in wasting three months of the year doing absolutely nothing. Watching windows, on balance looked like a good alternative, though I had to slap my face occasionally to stay awake.

What was more interesting than the window and what I imagined was going on behind the net curtains, however, was the little old lady that had been walking up and down the pavement across the road from where I was parked. Now this was strange. She had arrived a little after I had, and I didn't take much notice at first, but now I was getting curious. Was she looking for an address? Had she lost something valuable on the floor? Had she escaped from a mental institution? Was I so fed up and tired that I was imagining her?

I didn't want to draw attention to myself and go across to talk to her, but this was getting a bit ridiculous. I knew by instinct that if I left my car to see if I could be of any help that Evans would come strolling through the door, smelling of testosterone and drive off. This would ultimately mean that I wouldn't get paid.

For the record, my name is Morris Shannon, but everybody calls my Moggsy. I haven't been a private detective long enough to be any good at my job and the way things stand; maybe I am going to have to get myself something more financially secure like working in a factory, driving a taxi or pole dancing. Everybody said that I was a fool to start up my own business but as always I thought I knew what was best. The fact that it backfired good style is water under the bridge now, but even I didn't know just how bad life could become by following my selected career path. It certainly was a life changer and the job I was doing at the moment was just about as sad and badly paid as they come. From where I was sitting, working at the chicken packing factory on the Westhill Estate looked like an exciting vocational switch. At least, I would know at the end of the week there would be a wage packet waiting.

I had been hired by a freelance investigative reporter from down south called Tommy, to dig up some dirt on a local town councillor. This was going to be his big break into the tabloids, and I was doing all the legwork.

I had been tailing Councillor Evans for a week now, and his life could only be described a cesspool of seedy nightclubs, massage parlours, backhanders and now this. As the woman from the flat that I was watching drew the curtains, and her silhouette slipped out of her blouse and disappeared, I asked myself, just who it was that put these people in positions of power. Is it part of the job description for life in local politics, to be depraved, untrustworthy and money grabbing? I wondered what his wife would think when it hit the front pages of the nationals? To be fair, she seemed like a nice person; but him? For a middle-aged man, Evans certainly had a full lifestyle and just following him around was wearing me out. I went into my sandwich box and brought out a cheese and pickle. I hoped this lady got paid by the hour, not by the night.

CHAPTER THREE

The boys make a bee-line for the old lady. They're in no hurry now and in their own way want to savour the magic of the moment. This is going to be the highlight of the night; something to tell their mates about down the dole tomorrow. She's a bag lady, a fucking tramp no-mark; an easy target that needs a good kicking. It's a pity that she wasn't younger because they'd have thrown in a good shagging as well for free.

She's asking for it, and they are going to make sure she gets it. They've gone quiet now in blissful anticipation of the pleasure to come. The tallest of the bunch moves ahead of the pack. He's a skinhead with acute acne and is obviously the brains of the outfit, which isn't saying much for the rest. He stands blocking her path smirking inanely, but she makes no attempt to go around him. You see, she's savouring this moment too.

She stops but doesn't look him in the face just yet. She looks at her own washed out reflection in the wet window pane of the dry cleaners and cunningly watches him and his crew as they get ready to make their move.

"I can smell shit; you shit yourself, Ma?" The big soft lad known as Gaz laughs at his own feeble attempt at humour.

She's not laughing, but his crew are pissing themselves and high-fiving. They're running on wound up gang jibe and form a circle around her, so she can't get away. They're hyped up on power and ready to ejaculate their snarling unprovoked violence like a pack of hyenas on the savannah.

"Hey, wino; I'm talking to you." He's beginning to enjoy himself and like an actor in front of a captive audience, he struts in a bit closer, ready to make a grab for the bag. As he gets nearer, he realises that there is something wrong; nothing definite that he can put his finger on; just wrong. She's not giving the vibes he wants to be feeding off, and when she turns her head away from the window and makes eye contact for the first time, he can't help but stop. He forgets about the bag. Up close this old lady's face is all wrong too. It shouldn't be smiling and confident and eying him like he is the prey. It should be quivering with fear. His crew haven't picked up on it yet, but the big skinhead has the distinct impression that this isn't an old lady at all.

CHAPTER FOUR

I'd just finished off my last sandwich and was contemplating eating one of my partner Shoddy's homemade scotch eggs when I saw the scallies walking down Stanley Street on a collision course with the old dear. Even from where I was sitting they looked high on a cocktail of drugs and booze. The mindless chanting was something you got used to around these parts though they were chancing their luck on Stanley Street, which was an Everton stronghold.

The old lady was walking toward them like as if they weren't there. She was either short sighted, deaf or a friggin lunatic. Now this changes things. Fuck Evans and his tart, this was something a lot more serious, and could end up badly if things kicked-off, as I was pretty certain, they would.

What chance did she have against four pissed up no-marks who had nothing better to do? I didn't care now if Evans came out, drove off, or shagged himself to death. I couldn't just sit and watch the carnage. The scotch eggs were going to have to wait. I opened the door and stepped out. It made me realise that the inside of my car was colder than being on the street. I made a mental note to fix the heater next time I got paid. I reached into the back seat for my woolly scarf and trilby.

Neither the lads nor the old girl had noticed me yet, as I ambled toward them, and I quietly slipped my trusty metal knuckleduster over my left hand to even things up if it came to blows. I was pretty used to dealing with these types when I worked the doors at numerous clubs around the area. They were all mouth and bravado, but when it came down to it, didn't usually want to risk it against someone as big as me. I'm six feet four in my stocking feet and shaved my hair off years ago to give myself a kind of scary Yule Brynner, brick shithouse retro appeal. It impressed the ladies as well, which was a bit of an added bonus at the end of a long night shift.

My speciality back then was the screaming tank rush, which usually sent them scurrying off home via the chip shop, telling each other that they could have taken me at any time, but couldn't be arsed. I hoped it wasn't going to come to anything like that tonight, but I wasn't holding my breath, counting on it.

CHAPTER FIVE

"Go on, Gaz; let's see what she's got in her bag."

"Go on Gaz; She's asking for it."

"In the Bag, in the bag, in the bag, in the bag."

"In the Bag, in the bag, in the bag, in the bag."

The crew are egging him on, and even though he isn't sure anymore, Gaz isn't going to lose face in front of them. He makes a half-hearted lunge at it, but the old lady steps back takes a hatchet out and sinks it deep into his forehead. Before Gaz has hit the floor in a river of blood, like lighting, she catches another of his mates in the throat with the same axe, but this time leaves it buried in skin, bone and gore. It is beginning to look like a horror movie; Nightmare on Stanley Street with her as the director in charge of the action on set.

There's a shout in the distance and the sound of running feet, but it doesn't faze her. She puts her hand back in the bag and brings out a bloody great handgun this time. The two remaining scallies are running up Stanley Street for their lives; too shocked to have taken in what's happened.

She's in no rush now, though. The old lady rules the moment. She's playing God and has known all four were destined to die, from the first moment she set eyes on them. It's nothing personal; she isn't being selective here; it's random terror just for the sake of it. She savours the irony and sends a bullet that blows a hole you could put your fist through into the slowest, and then waits a couple of seconds. It looks like the only survivor is going to reach the corner. He quickens his pace making hysterical whimpering noises as he closes in on safety.

She's given him that slight hope on purpose but takes it away on a whim. She sends another bullet and takes off the back of his skull then turns her attention to the place where the shout originated from.

It's the fucking cavalry arriving to save the day. There's a huge man in an anorak running towards her with his arms outstretched yelling. He's clearly not very fit and looks pathetic and about as threatening as a Smurf. His trilby blows off, and she can see that he is bald. She fires a shot, which goes over his head, and he throws himself to the ground with a grunt. You get the feeling that this is more of a warning to stay away than any attempt at taking another life tonight.

She steps over the boys and drops a card on the one with the axe sticking out of his neck. He's certainly not chanting now. His body is still giving off small spasms like a chicken with no head as the last traces of life are extinguished. Job done!

She runs down the street with surprising agility and disappears around the corner onto Haswell Avenue.

There's an eerie silence hanging over Stanley Street like a shroud, but it doesn't last long. The spell is broken by the sound of a police siren in the distance getting louder, and flat windows being pulled up as people in their nightwear peer out to see what all the fuss is about.

CHAPTER SIX

"Let's go through this again, Shannon. What was the reason you were passing through Stanley Street, just as the attack took place?"

I was sitting in one of the interview rooms down at Croxley police station. It was closing in on nine o'clock in the morning, and I had been there since two am. Across the table was my old enemy DCI Jenkins, who as usual was dressed just one step up from a vagrant, in a dark, dishevelled suit that looked if it was a family hand-me-down antique, grungy red tie and brown pin-striped shirt. He was a fashion nightmare, and totally un-colour coordinated as was his sergeant, the Welsh Weasel, Harrison.

For once, I was in this room as a witness and not accused of anything and as if to emphasise this, I had been given a plastic cup of weak tea from the machine and a digestive biscuit, at about four in the morning.

I yawned and prepared myself to go through my story again for about the tenth time. "Like I said before, Mr Jenkins, I was driving through town, looking to see if the Golden Lantern was open as I was a bit peckish."

"That's a bit far away from your flat, Shannon. Why didn't you go somewhere local?"

"My partner Shoddy likes the spring rolls and authentic fortune cookies from there." Neither of them looked convinced, but I was not going to tell them the real reason I had been on Stanley Street that night. There is such a thing as client confidentiality even for private detectives.

"So let's hear it again from the top, about what you saw," said Harrison.

"Like I said, I was on my way to my favourite takeaway when I noticed a gang of four lads surrounding an old woman. Naturally, I stopped and got out of the car to go and help.

"Like any good law abiding citizen would do," sneered Harrison, in his North Wales drawl.

Shit! I hated this guy almost as much as I detested Jenkins. "Yeah that's right; I did what anyone would have done. I was walking over, and the next thing I knew all hell broke loose. The old woman pulled out an axe and attacked two of them with it. They went down, and the other two did a runner. I rushed towards them, and the old battleaxe pulls a bloody big gun from her bag, shoots the other two, and then takes a pot at me. I hit the floor, and by the time I had got back up on my feet she was gone.

I went over to see what I could do for the lads but...............well, you know the rest...I have never seen anything like that in my life before...........I don't want to again."

"So can you describe the woman?" Said Jenkins.

I shook my head. "I was too far away, and it all happened so quickly. She was carrying a big brown bag.

"How was she dressed?"

"Badly."

"How do you mean?" asked Harrison.

"She looked like an old tramp, but she certainly didn't move like one when she started doing her stuff with the axe. She must have run off pretty sharpish as well because I was only on the ground for no more than say twenty seconds."

"And you never thought about following her?" Said Harrison.

"Not being funny, but after what I had just witnessed, I wasn't about to give her a second chance at blowing my head off."

Jenkins went into a folder in front of him and brought out a blood-stained card. It was plain white with a poorly drawn Hangman. The crude sketch had a figure with just one leg and no arms. Underneath there were some letters and spaces.

N__ __ __ __ __ __   P__ __ __ __ __ A __

"Does this mean anything to you?"

"I don't know, should it?"

"Don't play silly buggers with us, lad," shouted Harrison.

"It's to do with a game that children play, where you have to guess what the word is before you get hanged isn't it?"

Jenkins nodded. "We found it on one of the bodies. Did you see the old lady put it there?"

"Nope."

Jenkins put the card back and stood up. He picked up the file and headed for the door. "That's all for now, Shannon, but don't leave the country, as we will be wanting to speak to you again sometime soon."

"I'll look forward to it, Mr Jenkins," I said to his disappearing back. "I don't suppose there is any chance of a lift back to my car is there, Mr Harrison?" From the look on the weasel's face, I got the impression that there wasn't.

CHAPTER SEVEN

The local paper has a front page spread that continues in the centre pages. The language is a bit theatrical even for the Echo, but incidents like this are rare in Croxley, and the Nationals have already smelt big news and sent their top reporters and cameramen. They are now in the process of interviewing just about anybody who lives in Stanley Street, and anybody who knew the victims. They're looking for the human angle; something sentimental. Basically, anything they can dig up that sells newspapers. The Echo feels under pressure from the big boys and is simply trying its hardest to compete in a race to ask the most inane questions possible. Even the big boys are already running out of any intelligent ideas. What they need is another multi-murder, and they have their fingers crossed and pencils poised.

It's a human tragedy, but good for business and the hotels and guest houses are full already, even though, it's only been a matter of hours. The police have cordoned off the whole street, which has irritated locals trying to get to work, as it means they have to take a big detour. Already there is the morbid procession of crime scene tourists arriving with their cameras and a thirst for the macabre. They come from all over and are literally falling over themselves to catch a glimpse of where it all took place. Blood patches left on the street would be a bonus. There's so much of the stuff on Stanley Street that it hasn't all been washed away yet.

Four murdered in horror axe attack

A brutal murder took place in the early hours of the morning as Croxley slept. Four young men in the prime of their life were slaughtered like animals while they headed home from the Red Lion Tavern on Clinton Street. They all died instantly: two from axe wounds and two from gunshots as they were running away.

The police are appealing for any witnesses and are following several lines of enquiries with an arrest imminent. They are keen to interview a woman carrying a large holdall, who was known to be walking in the vicinity of the crime scene.

Anyone who thinks that they may have seen this lady, described as old and shabbily dressed, should contact Croxley Police Station. No attempt should be made to engage her if she is seen, as she may be dangerous. The police will be making a statement later on in the day.

Inside the paper, there is lots of information on the boys, and interviews with neighbours and family members. The heading on the centre pages simply said: *Community in Shock asks why have our Boys been taken?*

When Mattie sees the headlines, he wants to punch the air with joy, but he holds himself back. It's been a long time since he's felt any joy in his life and he is a little out of practice. He takes a last puff from his cigarette, stumps it in the ashtray and slowly gets out of bed. Even after all these months, it is still painful to move too quickly. It's raining, and the gentle sound of the fine spray hitting the skyline of the bedroom can be plainly heard above the sound of his breakfast sizzling in the frying pan in the kitchen down the hall.

Mattie finds it difficult to dress himself these days. In fact, since the incident, he finds it difficult to do a lot of things. Without the use of one of his hands, and having only one eye working properly, life is not a barrel of laughs, but at least, the doctors saved his kidneys, and his back hadn't been broken as was first suspected. It's more of a mental thing that has changed the way he lives his life. He tends not to go out these days, especially after dark. Still, the news has cheered him up, and he pulls on his Levis and socks, tucks in his t-shirt and heads towards that delicious odour.

His girlfriend Erin is dishing out a plate of eggs, bacon and tomatoes. Mattie kisses her before he sits down, and gets a look of total disbelief. "What's that for?"

He hands her the paper. She reads it and lets out a sigh. "It couldn't have happened to a nicer bunch." She switches on the radio and tunes into the Croxley station. There's a local councillor called Evans, being interviewed about the attack. He has a reassuring soft voice and sounds convincing that the police have everything in hand and are closing in on an arrest.

"It's only a matter of time. Our community is special, and at this sad moment, I think that everyone is pulling together like they did during the war. We want our streets safe again for young and old, and while this maniac is on the loose, we need to all be especially vigilant. All I can say to everybody out there is that if anybody has information, let the police know. Boys like this are our future, and for them to be struck down like this is very sad; very sad indeed."

Erin sticks two fingers up at to the radio and switches it off. "Arsehole."

Mattie smiles for the second time that day; it always makes him laugh when Erin swears; it just doesn't seem right, and she usually goes bright red straight away after. Not this time, though. She comes over and cuts up his bacon for him.

"You'll be feeding me like a baby next. I'm not an invalid you know."

"Mattie?"

He knows what's coming, and he's ready for it.

"You didn't?.............well, ...you know?"

"I didn't what? ....Ah................I get it. Did I have anything to do with Gaz and his mates getting cut up? You've got to be joking, Luv. How about some coffee? If you're very lucky, I might take you out tonight to celebrate. There is no way I was involved, but it's the best news I've heard in months."

That seemed to satisfy her for the moment at least. She kisses him lightly on the cheek, walks over to the stove, puts the kettle on and tunes into Radio One.

CHAPTER EIGHT

I live in a dilapidated block of flats that were condemned as unfit for human inhabitation 20 years ago. I suppose in a way, the big loophole against getting re-housed somewhere even slightly more civilised is that most of the people that still live here, don't fit into any category I know, which could define them as human. Croxley is a hotbed of juvenile crime, and I live in its pumping heartland. The whole area is a throbbing open drain of drugs, prostitution and petty villainy. Violence is another of the traits that single it out as a five-star candidate for pulling down and starting again.   It has got so bad that the police don't even try anymore. They hid in lay-bys and book motorists for slight misdemeanours, to satisfy their bosses that they are working. It's pathetic really, but in my own way, I love the place and couldn't see myself surviving anywhere else.

The state of the streets should mean that there is a lot of work for a good private detective, but it's never seemed to have any positive effect on what I get offered. This leads me to conclude that it's most likely because I am not that good.

The brain of the operation is my partner Shoddy, and it was in his flat, which is next door to my own that I was now sitting drinking tea. Like everybody else within a 100-mile radius he had read the headlines, and was curious to know what the killing had all been about.

It was late morning, but he was still wearing his striped polyester pyjamas, and giving off his usual smell, which was a mixture of whiskey, self-rolled cigarettes, beer and boiled vegetables. The room was littered with cans and empty beer bottles, and I guessed that while I had been helping the police with their enquiries, he had been on a one man bender. He was always doing this, and I am used to it now. He was, after all, a raging alcoholic so what else could I expect.

Shoddy had a destitute look about him and his face an abandoned shipwreck quality that had the facility to shock people when they first met him. He had dark bags and crows feet under his intelligent but washed out blue-grey eyes, and his image was rounded off to perfection with grey receding dirty hair, missing front teeth and brown nicotine stained fingers.

Shoddy may have looked like he should have been under a pile of newspapers in a shop doorway, but when I first met him, he was a high-ranking police officer, who was well respected on the force and looked destined to get to the top. Even then, though, he must have had a destructive element built into his persona because an addiction to heroin and drink not only destroyed his career, it nearly killed him. He was discharged from his duties on grounds of ill-health.

These days the heroin is a distant memory even though, I know for sure that he still has the craving for a bag from time to time. He now keeps reality at bay with cheap booze, which he gets in bulk from the local supermarket. Shoddy may look and act like a vagrant and most of the time smell like one, but he still has one of the sharpest brains of anybody I have ever met. That's the reason he is my partner, and why I think we are the perfect team. He gets a buzz out of all of the routine boring work, which is a big part of the job, and without him, I would have definitely gone under long ago. When he is sober, he is a deadly tool I can use to help solve anything. He also has many contacts in the police and knows all of the crooks and villains around town, who still remember him how he was and respect him because of it.

"I tell you, Shod, the old woman was a lunatic. A simple surveillance operation and I almost get my head blown off. It's not worth the money or the aggro. I'm seriously thinking of jacking the whole thing in, and getting a job with the chicken people up on the West Hill Estate."

"So what about this Tommy character who hired you? Have you been in contact?"

"Aren't you listening, Shod? I'm telling you that I want to pack it in. If you had seen the blood and the state of those lads last night, I think you would be feeling the same."

Shoddy picked up the teapot and refilled my mug. "Couple of biscuits, mate?" He offered me the tin

"I think I need more than pissing, biscuits, Shod..Go on then, just a couple." I picked out a bourbon cream and a jammy dodger. He spooned some sugar into my mug and continued.

"It's just that I think you should see what the reporter Tommy has to say before you jack it in. It may be worth a bob or two. You were, after all, the only witness. Papers pay big money for something like that. It could see us all right for a couple of months or at least until another job turns up."

I dunked my biscuit into the tea, and the end fell off and floated around on top. Shoddy gave me a spoon to fish it out. "You're not having a good day are you, mate?"

"I gave Tommy a call when I got back to my flat; I'm going to see him this afternoon. I should type up a report about Councillor Evans and what he's been up to before we meet. That bastard is a sexual athlete. How the frig he got elected is beyond me. He's a con merchant."

"Nothing new there, Moggs. They're all at it down the town hall. You should have seen some of the things we were asked to turn a blind eye to when I was on the force. Speeding fines ripped up, one or two call girls beaten up and some right goings on with rent boys at private parties paid for by the taxpayers. It surprises me that any of that shower of twats had any time to do any work. Conservative, Labour and Liberal, they're all at it, mate; all tarred with the same shitty brush.

I looked at my watch; it was almost three o'clock. I had better get down to the office, finish off the report, and see what Tommy has to say. Are you down the pub tonight?" I didn't wait for the answer; it was a stupid question anyway. It was like asking the Pope if he was going to church on Sunday.

CHAPTER NINE

Mattie waits for Erin to go out to do the shopping before he dials the number. He has to be quick as he can only phone it between one o'clock and five past on a Tuesday or Thursday. He realises that it is very cloak and dagger, but it doesn't make him laugh or feel embarrassed. He respects the reasons why it has to be this way. He also knows the consequences for the person he is phoning if he gets found out.

As he is waiting for his call to be picked up, he looks out through the rain that has turned nasty and is now hammering against the kitchen window. Stretching out below him is the notorious West Hill Estate where you're either a villain or a victim. It's all extremes here with no middle ground. The 'Wessie,' is the definitive of living on the wrong side of the tracks. It's so far on the other side that the fucking tracks have long since disappeared, and even the police won't venture in after it goes dark.

Mattie and Erin live on the eighth floor of a ten-floor block that is identical to the other three that he can see from where he is standing. There's nothing nice about the place, but at least, until a few months ago he had thought that it was survivable. How wrong he had been, and how he longed to be able to escape. For people like him and Erin, though, there was very little chance of that. He couldn't see how he could live here very much longer. Not after what happened to his brother Jason; not after what happened to himself.

Someone has picked up the other end, and says a cautious, "hello." The voice is soft spoken and not from Merseyside. Mattie can hear the sound of traffic in the distance, and is curious as to where the other telephone is. He is sure it's a callbox in the middle of town; but which town?

He tries his best not to gush with gratitude and keeps it business-like and to the point. "I heard the news; I'm so happy."

"Where were you last night at midnight? Where you at home like I told you to be?"

"Yes, I was here with Erin all night."

"Good. This number is now obsolete. You can ring me at 051 4593259 any Thursday, Saturday or Monday at exactly 12 o'clock. Have you got your pen and paper? That's 051 4593259. Memorise it and destroy the paper." The line goes dead before he has the chance to ask the question that's been in his head since he got out of bed that morning. Does it end here? Has justice been served, or is this just the first course, with the main course still to come. They say that revenge is a dish, best-served cold, and now Mattie understands the significance.

There is the sound of a key turning in the lock, and Erin comes in. He hears her walking down the hall. She pops her head around the kitchen door. Her hair is wet, and she as looks beautiful as ever but doesn't look that happy. He hears other footsteps coming down the hall less delicate than those of his waif-like girlfriend. Two large men appear in the doorway wearing crumpled suits and carrying closed umbrellas which drip water onto the fake wood effect hallway floor. They don't look very friendly, even though they are attempting to smile; but there again why should they? He knows who they are and why they have come. He doesn't need Erin to explain, but she does anyway.

"Mattie, it's the police. They say that they want to have a quick word."

CHAPTER TEN

By four o'clock I was sitting in my office with a badly typed report in my hand and a non-itemised bill for my services waiting for Tommy to arrive. I was going to add on a couple of quid for the stress of getting caught up in a murder but thought it best to leave it to his discretion. I intended to slip it in somewhere in our conversation. My small office is on Croxley High Street, above a betting shop and paid for by the allowance that I got off my dad, who is a retired millionaire.

After all attempts had failed to get me to enter the family used car business, my dad sold it and moved to Spain with mum. It was her that persuaded the mean old sod to pay money into my bank every month, but it barely covers the rent on my council flat and the one room that I work out of. Without this money and Shoddy's small police pension, we would have been back on the dole a long time ago. Dad said that because I didn't have any brothers or sisters, I would inherit the lot in the end, but as he intended to live a long life, I would just have to be patient. That was his revenge on me for not conforming, and at the end of the day; I couldn't blame the old git.

Tommy arrived half an hour late. He was a tall, thin bloke with hippy brown hair tied back in a pony-tail and a frigging earring in the shape of a cross, dangling from his left ear. He always looked permanently wired and under pressure, and I wondered whether this was drugs induced or just his natural mental state. Tommy was an incessant smoker and nail biter and was dressed very snazzy in a three-piece brown herringbone suit that looked tailor made and expensive.

He's a cockney sparrow, and I got the distinct impression that he only listened to the bits I said that he wanted to hear, and he just tuned out the rest and listened to another channel in his head. Taking to Tommy was like being verbally assaulted. He hit you with questions, filed away your answers and hit you some more.

He read my report quickly and then threw it on my desk.

"So our friend Evans has been putting it about a bit, Moray."

"It certainly looks like it, Tom, and that's Moggsy by the way."

"If we're going to play that game, Moggsy, let's stick with Tommy then eh?"

I passed him my bill for the work I had done, and fair play to the guy, he took the money out of his wallet and passed it over. I made a half-hearted attempt to look for the change, but he told me to skip it, and lit up yet another cigarette with the stub of the one he had just been smoking. Bloody marvellous; I hate cigarette smoke, and it looked like the office was going to reek of it for days. It wasn't normal smoke either; he was smoking small untipped cigarettes that smelt like as if they were Turkish. He saw me looking at the packet and offered me one. I refused got up and opened the window to give him the hint. It wasn't taken. I frigging hate Cockneys.

"So what do you want me to do with Evans? Do I keep on following him?"

"Forget Evans for now. You must be the only person in town who got a look at this woman who cut up the four kids. That kinda makes you exclusive, Moggsy. How about you tell me the story of what happened, and we will leave Evans on the shelf. He's always going to be a good story, but this murder is hot, and everyone is talking about it."

"How much?"

"You what?"

"If I'm so exclusive, how much are you going to give me to tell you what happened?"

"That depends, old son."

"Depends on what?"

"That depends on how much you saw, and how much I can get for writing a fucking good column."

"So what figures are we talking here, Tommy?"

He brought out a notebook, wrote something on the front page, tore it off and passed it across the desk to me. "Look, I can give you that for now, and maybe there will be more if I get lucky. What do you say, Moggsy? Are we on?"

I looked at the figure and whistled internally, but kept my face neutral. "Is that all?"

"I can add a zero on that if you give me the information, and I get a big newspaper interested in printing it, but that's all that I can do, and I can't promise anything. What I can say, though, is that I think this is a story that has got a lot of mileage, and I want to approach it differently from the other guys in the paparazzi. There could be more work in it for you. If we get lucky, this could be the jackpot, Moggsy; what do you say?"

It didn't need thinking about. "Okay Tommy, I'll take you at your word. "What do you want to know?"

CHAPTER ELEVEN

From the kitchen doorway where he is standing with Sergeant Harrison, DCI Jenkins can see that Mathew Webster or Mattie as he likes to be known looks a lot better than the last time that he saw him. Okay, so he doesn't have the use of one of his hands and one of his eyes has a patch over it, but compared to that hospital visit not long after he had been beaten up, he looked like a different person.

He's still got that frightened look on his face, though, but who wouldn't have after what he has been through. After being beaten close to death, he was thrown over a wall and was lying there for hours before the alarm was raised by a man driving a milk float.

Erin directs then into a small lounge that just about takes the three piece suite, television and dining room table. It's a tight squeeze, but they all manage to sit down. There's a hostile atmosphere present in the room between the two police officers and the couple, which you would have to be stupid or completely insensitive not to notice.

DCI Jenkins gets himself comfortable in the cheap fake leather armchair, shifts his fat around and leans forward slightly to address Mattie. He is trying to blot Erin out and wishes she hadn't followed them in, but she sits on the arm rest and puts her hand on her boyfriend's shoulder as if to protect him.

"You know why I'm here, Mattie." It wasn't a question; it was a statement of fact.

"We know what's happened, Mr Jenkins if that's what you mean. We don't need you to come around here to bring us the news personally." Erin tries to keep an element of calm in her voice but fails miserably.

"Those bastards deserved everything they got," said Mattie, avoiding eye contact and putting his one good arm around Erin's waist. Her face is now red with fury as if she is ready to explode.

"If you know all that," continues Jenkins, then you know what my obvious question has to be, and the reason why I'm here."

Mattie shakes his head and smiles in mock amusement. "I was in the house all last night. We watched a film didn't we, love."

"Any other witnesses?" said Jenkins

"No, we were on our own." He looks at his girlfriend for support.

Erin nods her head to confirm Mattie was with her. She looks at Jenkins and Harrison with contempt. "After what those scumbags did to Mattie and Jason, could you blame us for being happy at what happened? That doesn't mean that we are guilty of doing anything. It just confirms that there is a God, and wherever he is, he is watching.

"I don't think that it was God that killed Gaz and his mates," interrupted Harrison. This was definitely some kind of revenge mission, and the only person that has got a big enough grudge to kill them is you, Mattie."

Erin gets up from the chair. "I think you've said enough. You were useless back then at trying put those four behind bars, and now, you have the cheek to come around here looking for an easy arrest. That's all you people ever think about. You go for the easy option. To me, you're as bad as Gaz and the other three. The good thing now is that they won't be bothering anybody else."

Harrison ignored the outburst and concentrated on Mattie. "You were a bit of a tearaway yourself before you got hurt. You didn't mind beating someone up if the price was right. You were a bit of a hard knock, Mattie. Didn't you want to get revenge?"

"He didn't do nothing," screamed Erin "All we want now is to get on with our lives and stop being hassled for things that we didn't do."

"Well I can't guarantee that," said Jenkins lifting himself up from the armchair. "This is a very serious murder enquiry, and we are trying to piece together why this incident occurred and who was the instigator. I wouldn't be doing my job properly if I didn't pursue every line of enquiry. Thank you for speaking to us, but we may want to talk to you again Mattie."

"Either here or down at the station if your girlfriend continues with her attitude," interrupted Harrison.

"Fuck off out of my house." Erin is furious now and strides into the hallway her eyes hot and red with tears.

The police officers calmly follow her and go through the front door that she opens and then slams shut behind their disappearing backs.

The go down in the lift that smells of urine, and outside in the car park get into an unmarked dark blue Ford Cortina. The rain has stopped now, and the sun is trying to break through the low clouds scurrying across the estate. Jenkins sits in the passenger seat and lights his pipe. It's taking him a long time to get it going the way he wants it, but the whole process seems to relax him. Harrison drives out into the light afternoon traffic and heads in the direction of Croxley Police Station. He, in turn, lights up a Players Number Six. "I can't see either of them capable of something like that, sir."

"Yeah, not a bloody chance, sergeant. It's not a question of barking up the wrong tree. On this one, we're not even in the right forest."

CHAPTER TWELVE

Dark Angel of Death Could Have Superhuman Powers

Eyewitness spills the beans

By Thomas Brand

It's not often that a special agent comes up against the unexplainable, but it seems that the only witness to the atrocious attack on four unarmed youths, walking through Croxley in Merseyside, has not ruled out the possibility of mysterious powers at work. Our witness works in the shady undercover world of the 'super spy' and knows that there is so much more going on behind the scene in our security forces than anyone will admit too.

As a special favour, I was granted an interview with a man so high up in security that there are no records that he actually exists; a man that makes James Bond look second rate that has missed death himself by seconds on that bloody night. I met the agent who goes by the codename MO, at a secret location, and during our time together he explained what happened that fateful night when the streets of sleepy Croxley run red with the blood of four of its young men that had seemingly done nothing wrong.

MO explained that he was in Stanley Street purely by chance that evening, on an important undercover operation that was Top Secret. He noticed the old lady walking up the street carrying what he assumed was a normal handbag, but what he later found out to be a portal into a world of death, destruction and despair.

The four local lads, who had been for a night out with friends that evening, were observed by our agent laughing and singing, as they walked toward the old lady. As they got closer, a transformation took place. I was informed that there was a blinding light, and she transformed in front of his eyes into what he could only describe as a lethal killing machine. In his own words, he described the being that was at work in front of him as like a 'Dark Angel' because she seemed to float as she took the lives of these four unlucky young adults.

"I ran toward the scene of the destruction, but she raised her hand in a gesture, and I was hit by a powerful blow that seemed to come out of the air. I was thrown backwards and hit the ground hard, losing consciousness. When I came around, I just caught sight of something I can only describe as looking like a 'Dark Angel' travelling at lightning speed and then disappearing. I thought that I had been hallucinating at first, but when I heard the police sirens I realised that it had all been real."

MO is not what you would call your average sort of witness, but is a highly trained professional that is not open to making exaggerated claims. The fact that he witnessed what seems to be an old lady transform into a killing machine could turn out to be one of the great unsolved mysteries, or possibly could be something that *reoccurs again. If there is even the slightest possibility, then it is up to the general public of Croxley to keep on their guard and tell the police if they see anything suspicious.*

So who is the Dark Angel? Could she be some new type of automated Android that has been developed behind the iron curtain? Or is she so Top Secret that nobody in government wants to give away her true identity. Maybe she is not of this earth?

The only theory that special agent MO put forward was that maybe this was an experiment in bionic limbs that went wrong, and the robot that was created was so powerful that it escaped. If this is the case, then it is possible that it could morph into other strange shapes. The truth could be even stranger, and we now wait with baited breath to see if anymore incidents occur.

"Bloody Hell," said Shoddy as he threw the newspaper onto the table and made his way to the teapot to pour us both another cup of tea. "That's a bit over the top even for the usual rubbish that paper usually churns out. That's not news; it's a bleeding fairy story; fucking robots and bionic arms. What the Hell did you tell that reporter, mate?"

"He made the whole thing up. I told him what I saw, and he changed it so that it makes no sense."

We were sitting in Shoddy's flat, and I was furious. I had been looking forward to going down the pub for my usual Sunday morning drink and had noticed the headlines as I passed the newsagents. As I was the only eyewitness I was curious to see what I was supposed to have seen, but what I read took away my thirst and I had headed back home and woke Shoddy up.

I took a sip of tea. "I suppose that you can expect anything from a newspaper that claims Elvis is still alive and living with aliens."

"So how much did you get for the story?"

"Not enough obviously, this may be a shit paper, but it is read by a lot of people all over the country, and I wouldn't bet against Tommy getting ten times more than he paid me."

"So what are you going to do now, Moggs?"

"Do? I'm going to go round to his house and hit the little git; that's what I'm going to do."

"So where does he live?"

It was only then that I realised I didn't know. "On second thoughts, I'm going to ring him up and get to the bottom of it on the phone." I found the number I had been given, in my notebook and dialled. Tommy picked up almost instantly.

"You've got a damned cheek Tommy; what the hell do you think you're playing at coming up with a story like that?"

"I know, Moggs, I honestly believe I could have come up with a better name than the Dark Angel, but Supergran is already a kids television program, and I couldn't have used Supertramp for obvious reasons."

"I don't mean that you daft sod; how come you made the whole story up? Robots, bionic arms and possible alien connections; it's a pack of absolute rubbish."

"Oh, that. It's called poetic licence, Moggs, and don't worry because every reporter does it to a certain extent. It's what is known in the trade as an eye catcher. A sort of aperitif to get people interested. If other nationals and local television and radio stations pick up on the Dark Angel bit, then we are quid's in, mate."

"Don't mate me you, bastard. Why do people read the trash that they print in that rag?"

"Well, you read it didn't you? Anyway enough of this, we have more important things to discuss, and I am assuming here that you have heard the news this morning?"

"What news?"

"Oh Good God, Morris, you really are so slow to be a detective. Turn on any radio or television, and they are all talking about it. Even now at this early stage, I have heard her called the Dark Angel, or Angel."

"What about her?"

"She's struck again, old son. Have a listen and ring me back. We have a lot of work to do."

CHAPTER THIRTEEN

There are two entrances to the Havana Club in Lord Street, Wellston, which is about as posh an area as you get in Croxley. The discreet entrance at the front leads directly onto the road and is what most of the punters use when visiting this most exclusive of men's clubs, but there is another one around the back that is reserved for 'extra special' people.

It is three of these 'extra special' people that are leaving the Havana this Saturday night by the back door. They make their way through the ornate, but fake Victorian garden, towards the wooden gate that leads into an even more discreet alley at the back of the club. This is where they had parked their Jaguars and Daimlers earlier on in the evening. The men are all dressed in suits and dark Crombies and saunter slowly down the path, at peace with themselves after enjoying the delights of some of the young teenage girls and boys on offer for a price, on the first floor of the club.

That first floor has the five bedrooms that most of the club's membership never sees because it is out of their price league. Most of the all-male membership content themselves with buying overpriced champagne for the club's hostesses, and stuffing money down the bras and panties of good looking lap dancers that are hired from off the estates that they can watch squirming around half-naked in front of them, but must never touch. The Havana is the ultimate hard on for the well-off professional set of Croxley, but the real action takes place upstairs, and here, anything goes.

One of the men stops to relieve his bursting bladder in a bush, and the other two stand around on the concrete path, smoking their cigars waiting for him to finish. He takes a long time to get started, and he smiles to himself at how difficult it is to piss after three hours of depraved sex. Two young lads and a girl all for himself; it was expensive, but he deserved it, after all of the hard work he had been putting in recently. Those kids off the estates were like farmyard animals; they didn't seem to mind what you did to them or what they did to you as long as they got paid.

It's a beautiful evening for the time of year and the midnight sky is cloudless and full of stars. The moon is almost full and bright enough for one of the men, who just happens to be a high-ranking police officer, to pick up the silhouette of something very strange by the closed wooden gate leading to the alley.

"Anybody ordered a goodnight wank before we go home?" he blurts out to nobody in particular,"

"Why? Got something in mind, Joe?" said the eminent local councillor, finally zipping up his fly.

"How about that one over there, boys?"

All three men are now focused on the figure half in shadow and half caught by the moonlight, leaning against the wall by the closed gate. She is naked from the waist up, and the moonlight glistens off her bare breasts. Her face is in shadow, but she has long black hair that falls down to her black leather mini-skirt. Her outfit is finished off with fishnet stockings and knee length black stiletto boots.

The men are captivated by the size of her breasts and don't notice the large brown bag at her feet because a bush partly conceals it.

"Feeling hungry lass? How about coming and sucking on this," says the high-ranking police officer. This makes the other two laugh out loud.

"Room on top for all three, love," said the local councillor not wanting to be outdone. The men are moving toward her now, not really understanding why this gorgeous creature is half naked in front of them, but they are being led by their dicks, not their brains, and are going to take full advantage of the situation. This is going to round the evening off nicely.

The girl gets down on her knees and bows her head in a submissive sexual position, waiting for them. The high ranking police officer already has a hard on even though he has just screwed a fifteen-year-old less than half an hour ago. He can't believe his luck and walks faster than the other two so that he is first. Unfortunately for him, his luck is about to change.

As he comes up close to the girl's bowed head, he unzips his trousers and says, "How about sucking on this, darling, for starters?"

The girl raises her head. "I can do better than that." The voice is just a whisper, but it's deep and obviously that of a man. He doesn't see the knife as it slices through his penis, and doesn't feel any pain initially because his body is pumping endorphins. It is still pumping as the figure drives the long bladed knife up through his neck and into his brain.

The other two men are far enough behind so as not to have a definite idea of what's going on, but when they see the first man fall back and land on the path with empty staring eyes, they freeze. Before they have time to react, it's all over. The figure in front of them raises a revolver with a silencer and shoots them both through the head. Even before they stop twitching the figure peels of the fake soft silicone breast suit, and gets to work.

CHAPTER FOURTEEN

As soon as I heard the news about the three men that have been murdered I rang Tommy back, and we arrange to meet at the office later on that morning. Tommy arrived almost an hour late and was on his second cigarette in the time it took me to make him some tea. He looked wired-up like he hadn't slept for days but seemed pleased at the events of the night before. This made me feel a bit sickened for obvious reasons.

"I was waiting for the next one to happen, Moggsy. I tell you this is going to be huge news and could make me a fortune if I play my cards right." He caught the look that I gave him. "You are going to be quid's in yourself, mate, but we need to get our act together before somebody beats us to it."

"What's with this 'we' Tommy? I don't remember agreeing to anything. I just told you the story about what I saw, when those lads were murdered, and you twisted all of that, so it was just a load of lies."

"Wise up, man." He lit his third cigarette with the stump of the other. "People are getting murdered every day. The fact that this lady is doing it in a spectacular way makes it different. If we can get closer to the action, then the national newspapers are going to be handing out loads of money with their tongues hanging out for more copy."

"How do you mean, get closer to the action?"

"What we have here is a load of reporters arriving in town and picking up a story about a person who likes to kill in a very strange, sort of artistic way. You heard about those three men, and what she did to them didn't you?"

I nodded.

"Well at the moment, all of those reporters that have arrived will be rushing around trying to look for an angle. But they don't have any local knowledge, and it is going to take them a while to get it together."

"What about the local reporters? They have got all of the local knowledge about who the victims were."

"Forget the local reporters, Moggsy; they are all shit because otherwise they would be working for a national. We have only got a little bit of time, but what I want you to do, is work for me to dig out a very special angle on this."

"Oh yeah. What do you mean by that?"

""I want you to help me track the Dark Angel down, so I can do an interview with her."

I almost spat my tea out. "You must be crazy Tommy. How do you think that I am going to do that when you have the police with all of their recourses totally baffled?"

"I want to hire you like anybody else would so that you can get to the bottom of this. The angle that we are going to use is that I am going to write about what we have been doing to track down the Angel. That's got to be worth a load of money off one of the nationals, and it's going to be read by the whole country every morning. I want it to culminate in my interview with her so that I can find out what her motives are."

"But don't we have an obligation to turn her over to the police?"

"Eh? Yes, Yes, of course, Moggsy. But when we find her, I want that exclusive interview first, and then you can do what you like."

"No pressure there, then."

"I don't think you are treating this as serious as you should. Think yourself lucky that you are in the right place at the right time. If you do your job properly, you will make a load of money............"

"So will you."

"Yeah that's right; we are both going to benefit from this when we find the killer. What do you say, Morris?"

"I say you are a friggin nutter."
"Joking apart?"

"Joking apart, I still say that you are off your head. And what's with this 'when,' business, about finding the killer? Surely you should be saying if?"

"I have confidence in you Morris."

"My arse, you have."

"Ok, let's talk cash, Moggsy. How much do you want to help me track down the Dark Angel?"

"So, you're settled on that name then?"

"Yes."

"It sounds a bit shit to me."

"Well that's your opinion, and you are entitled to it."

"Why is she dark?"

"That's her soul."

"Angel?"

"How the fuck do I know, it just sounded right. So are we on or not?"

"I can't give you any guarantee that I will be able to find her."

"No problem."

"I'm not saying that even if I do find out who she is that I could set it up for you to do an interview."

"No problem; just try your best."

"Well..........I can't promise anything..."

"You've already said that, Moggsy. Are we on or not?"

"That depends."

"Depends on what?"

"Let's talk money, and we'll take it from there."

Tommy rubbed his hands together. "You're a capitalist Morris. I like that. If it just comes down to money, then you're talking my kind of language. Let's get down to what really matters. How much do you want?"

"Well................... There is going to be a lot of expenses up front............... My partner needs paying too.......................I might need some funds to pay people for information..............How about...................."

CHAPTER FIFTEEN

Another Savage Attack by the Dark Angel

Thomas Brand

The police were being tight-lipped this morning after another savage attack by the so-called Dark Angel. The brutal assault that led to the death of three well-known local men took place in the garden of the Havana Club, which is situated in the Wellston district of Croxley. As yet the three men have not been named but what we have learnt is that the bodies have been dismembered in some kind of ritualistic cult ceremony. This is believed to have taken place after they were dead. The murderer is thought to be highly unstable and extremely dangerous to the public.

The Havana is known to be an exclusive gentleman's club, popular with local businessmen and dignitaries. In a brief statement from the police, it was confirmed the attacker was the same one who carried out the murder of the four young men in Stanley Street last week. DCI Jenkins, who is leading the investigation, said that there were no witnesses to the incident and that his crime squad were now working on a number of leads.

It seems that the Dark Angel is able to appear at will, and has enough power to overcome her victims even though she is outnumbered. There is obviously concern in the community about where she will strike next, and that's why everybody is now taking extra care, and making sure that they are not alone walking through the streets of Croxley at night.

The truth about why and how this apparition is able to terrorise a community is not clear, and already the town is full of rumours as to what the motive is. Could it be revenge attacks? Could the Dark Angel be simply choosing victims at random in a sort of crazy death game? Whatever the reasons are, one thing is certain, and that is that the police are baffled, and maybe just like Jack the Ripper, the true identity of this enigma may never be known.

We all pray that this is the last of the attacks, and our sympathy and prayers go out to the families and loved ones of the deceased.

Mattie throws the newspaper onto the table and takes a bite of his toast. Erin is flicking from station to station on the radio to try and get some up to the minute news about the triple murder.

Even though Mattie doesn't know who the three men were that had been walking through the garden that night, he knew what they stood for, and also that he hated them. Both he and Erin knew all about what went on at the Havana, in the upstairs rooms, and it was the reason he had ended up semi-disabled, and his brother Jason had been killed. Mattie was no stranger to the shady underground gangland world around Croxley and Merseyside, and nobody could ever accuse him of being naive. He was, however, naive enough not to have noticed the slow decline of his brother, into heroin addiction, and hated himself for this. Even when he had eventually found out about it, and learnt how his brother was funding the habit, he still chose to do nothing. When Jason eventually was found dead, floating in the canal, it was too late, and the revenge that he planned was never going to work against the people that he was up against. The only lucky thing that had happened to him in the past six months was the fact that he was still alive. He looked at the two suitcases at the side of the television for him and Erin. He knew that if the police could work out the obvious connection between him and the murder of Gaz and his mates, then so would a lot of other people. He knew that he had to get out, and only hoped that he hadn't left it too late.

He looked at the time, waited for thirty seconds and then dialled the number.

"Hello." The voice at the other end of the line is cautious and soft-spoken.

"It's me. I heard the news about the Havana. Does it end here or is there more?"

"There is more."

"I took your advice, and we are leaving at two o'clock this afternoon for Scotland. I have a relative in Motherwell."

"This won't be for long. It will soon be over and safe for you to come back."

"How will I know?"

"Oh, you'll know alright. Just keep checking the papers. Remember the favour that you need to do for me? I will call you when I need it."

"You know that I can never repay you for what you have done...........................Hello......."

"Make sure that you are on that train, Mathew." The line goes dead. That was the first time the voice on the other end of the phone had used his name. Nobody ever called him Mathew. It was strange, but when he heard that calm voice on the phone, it made him feel safe. He didn't like change, and leaving his flat and making the long trip to Glasgow was not something he was looking forward to. Still, he had very little choice if he wanted to stay alive. He also had Erin to consider. What would these bastards do to her if they thought that he knew anything? He shuddered. There was a knock on the door, and he jumped back into reality.

Erin got up to answer

"Leave it," he said. "It's got to be bad news no matter who it is."

"It could be my mum," said Erin. "She said that she would come around to see us before we go. If it was anybody bad, do you think that they would knock?"

Mattie nodded. "Yeah, those bastards would just kick the door in."

She disappeared down the hall and came back seconds later.

"Mattie, there's a man here that wants a word with you. He says his name in Morris Shannon, and that he is a private detective. Shall I ask him to come in?"

CHAPTER SIXTEEN

As soon as I got back to Shoddy's place after meeting with Tommy, we got to work. I had insisted on some money up front, and even though I was tempted to go to the pub with it and take the rest of the day off, I resisted.

The police had been scant in giving out information about the three people killed though they had indicated that there was some mutilation of the bodies. We had to find out exactly what had happened and hand over the information to Tommy so he could weave his magic, and sell it to the highest bidder. In the end, all that it took was a trip down to the Croxley police station by Shoddy, and a lunchtime drink with some of his old buddies, to get more than enough information to justify our fee.

That evening, we went out to the pub and held our meeting there. The Old One Hundred is only a short stagger away from my flat. It's not one of those modern chic city pubs that are springing up everywhere these days, but it's the type of establishment where you can have a serious drink, in the company of serious drinkers. Shoddy has his own tankard that the landlord Bill keeps behind the bar for him, and I have my favourite seat, in the snug. This is a little room off the main bar area, with a scattering of rough looking, heavy duty green leather armchairs and some tables that could give you some severe splinters if you didn't treat them with respect. Around the walls, there are pictures of soldiers from the First World War, which must be some significant factor on how the pub got its name, but nobody I have ever spoken to knows what the connection is.

The Hundred hadn't seen a lick of paint in my lifetime, and the old-time ambiance and violent vibe at closing time is the main reason students and trendies stay well clear, preferring the new wine bar across the street, or a bus into Liverpool. I love the pub because the beer is cheap; the decor doesn't make you feel out of place, plus it is next door to a fish and chip shop, so in my world ticks all of the boxes.

I placed Shoddy's first pint of the evening in front of him and settled down in my favourite chair. "So what did you turn up about the Havana, mate?"

He took his time, lit up a cigarette, drained half of his drink down to the half way mark, then wiped the froth off his lips. "It's bloody terrible what's happened to those three. I tell you, mate; this is a monster that we are dealing with. If this Tommy character thinks you can get him an interview, he must be off his head."

"Correction, Shod, I need my head testing to have agreed to it."

"You should have asked for more money."

"Tommy said that if we got it right, then the money would come rolling in for all of us."

"Yeah, but it's not him that's putting his neck on the line. This character is dangerous. Dark Angel my arse; what she did even made some of the local lads down at the station vomit, and they are a hard shower of bastards."

"Fill me in."

He unbuttoned his coat and reached into his trouser pocket, revealing that underneath he was still wearing his pyjamas.

"Are you ready for bed, Shod?"

He didn't rise to the bait, but brought out a piece of paper and smoothed it out on the table. The three men killed were Joe Blake, William Jones and Cyril Blackmore. Blake was a Police Superintendent and the other two Croxley Councillors.

I whistled. "So they were pretty big fish then. What were they doing at the Havana?"

"It's one of those posh gentlemen's clubs that has a membership fee that is more than we earn in a month. It's full of rich tossers and half of the local council."

"So what's the crack with the club?"

"No crack, Moggs, it is a legitimate business that's as clean as a whistle. Apparently these three had been there for a couple of hours, had dinner, a few drinks and were on their way home. They were walking through the back garden to pick up their cars when the attack happened."

"Why the back garden?"

"I wasn't given any reason, but as there are double yellow lines at the front, it is where they had parked their cars."

"So what happened?"

"Blake had a long blade knife driven up through his neck and into his brain. He must have died instantly. The other two were shot in the head. It doesn't stop there, though. One of the councillors, Blackmore I think, was left hanging from a tree by a noose........"

"The hangman element, again."

Shoddy nodded. "Yeah, and get this; the policeman Blake had his cock chopped off and stuffed in his mouth, and the remaining bloke William Jones had been stripped naked and was wearing a false silicone body-top with a pair of breasts."

"You are having me on, Shod."

"I kid you not, son. There was fucking carnage in that garden, and to top it all, another hangman card was left on Jones's body." He went into his pocket and brought out a piece of paper. "There was a hangman with two legs and no arms, and look at the writing underneath."

N __ __ H __ __ __   P __ __ S __ __ A __ L

I couldn't make out what the two words were meant to say, but noted that the figure now had two legs. "So what's it all about? What the Hell is she trying to say, Shod?"

"Who knows, mate. Nobody down the station has got a clue either, but they are worried that it's going to happen again. The fact that the figure now has two legs could mean that there is going to be another two killings."

"What's with the silicone breasts?"

"I haven't got a clue, Moggs. I didn't even know that such things existed, but I saw the pictures taken by the police cameraman, and I have to say that they look like the real thing from a distance. You strap the suit onto your chest. Apparently it's all the rage for transvestites."

"So is the killer trying to say that this councillor was a transvestite?"

"Your guess is as good as mine, but nobody knows a thing. They are attempting to find a link between the three men killed at the Havana and the four lads, but nobody has come up with any ideas yet. Still, what we have should be enough for Tommy to be going on with, so we can justify our wages. There's more as well. DCI Jenkins has identified a local villain, who may have an axe to grind with those four lads. Six months ago he was beaten up and left for dead, and he claimed it was this gang that did it. There is also the fact that his brother was found dead, floating in the can that could also be relevant."

"What's his name Shod?"

"Mathew Webster. If you want to go around and see him, I have his address as well. I'm going back to see the lads tomorrow, to see if I can dig up some more information on him and if there is any dirt on the three men that were killed."

Before I went home, I used the pub telephone and gave Tommy all of the news about the murder. He seemed pleased at what we had got and told me to look out for it in the paper the next day. I left it at that and didn't tell him that I was going to interview a suspect that was linked to the killings. That could keep until later. I didn't want to give him too much in one go, but drip feed him to keep the flow of money coming in.

The next morning, I caught the newspaper headlines before making my way to see Webster. I was surprised that Tommy had not exaggerated as much this time and Shoddy also drew my attention to the fact that even though I had told him about the hangman card left at the scenes of both murders, he hadn't written anything about it. Shoddy was under the impression that it probably didn't fit in with the profile of a Dark Angel, or that he could be saving it to release as a bombshell in a later edition. The fact that no other newspapers, either local or national had got this piece of information was also something strange. If Tommy had this advantage, why wasn't he using it?

Mathew Webster lived right in the centre of the West Hill Estate, which is a hotbed of every type of crime you can think of, and is inhabited by the lowlife of Croxley. It's gangland rule here, and most of the gang members are teenagers. As I parked my car up, I was glad that I only drove a decrepit Riley Elf, as it blended in well with all of the wrecked cars with their windows smashed and flat tyres that were scattered around the concrete area that served as a car park. I headed towards the block of flats where Webster lived and noted the gang of lads hanging around on the corner watching me. They were checking me out and wondering what I was. The fact that I was wearing a suit, anorak and trilby was unusual around these parts. This set me apart as either police or insurance salesman. Either wasn't welcome, but as it was still daylight I was probably not going to get any trouble. After dark, it would have been a completely different story,

The lift wasn't working, so I made my way up the steps to the balcony that housed number eleven and knocked the door. Nobody answered at first and then a thin-faced lady with short dyed blonde hair answered and scowled at me. I assumed that this was Webster's girlfriend. She was dressed in a shell suit that was shiny turquoise and had fluffy bright red slippers on her feet. I gave her my card. She took it and shut the door in my face without saying a word. I waited...........and waited, and was just about to give up when she came back and stepped to one side, which I assumed was her way of saying that I could come in.

Mathew Webster was sitting at the kitchen table with a mug of tea in his hand. He was blonde like the girl who had answered the door and had a patch over his right eye. He was dressed in jeans and a T-shirt and didn't look too pleased to see me.

"Mr Webster?" The girl who had answered the door came into the room and sat down. It was her who spoke.

"We've said all that we have to say to the police. What do you want with us?

"I'm sorry to disturb, but I'm working for a client who has an interest in the murders that happened in Stanley Street and at the Havana."

"Are you working for any of those slags that got done in?" Said Webster.

"No, I've just been hired by a newspaper reporter to get to the bottom of it. He wants to know why these people have been killed and what the link is."

"So what's that got to do with us?" asked Webster."

"Didn't you have some trouble with the four lads that were killed?"

"You mean this," he said holding up his hand.

"If you like. They gave you a bit of a kicking I hear. I bet you were well pleased when you heard what had happened to them."

"That doesn't mean that I had anything to do with it."

"I never said that it did. You must have been happy though because I know I would have been if they had done that to me."

"Yeah, but we were here all night when they got done over; ain't that right, Luv?" he put his good arm around his girlfriend.

"Look Mathew..............."

"That's Mattie; only me ma calls me Mathew."

"OK, look, Mattie, I don't give a toss about those lads because they probably deserved it, but the bloke I'm working for, thinks he can get us all some money by finding out why these people are being killed." It was at this stage I introduced the pound notes. I put a little pile of twenties on the table. "We can all do with a bit of money, can't we, Mattie. How about some information? I can assure you that your name is not going to be mentioned."

The girl looked at Mattie, got up and went over to the cooker. "I'm Erin by the way; do you want a cup of tea?" she smiled, but it didn't reach her eyes, which were dull and lifeless.

"I'd love one, Erin."

"You'd better sit down then. Mattie, stick that money in your trousers, let's call it a bit of compensation for our suffering.

He reached out, counted it and put it in his pocket. "So what do you want to know?

"Did those lads have anything to do with what happened to your brother?" I thought he was going to throw his tea over me, but the anger that I saw in his eyes for a second disappeared, as Erin came back and handed me a mug of colourless liquid.

"Sorry, we are out of sugar..............and teabags. I had to use an old one."

"That's no problem; I'm always doing that myself." I looked at Mattie, expectantly."

"If you want to know what happened to Jason, you had better start investigating what goes on at the Havana club on the second floor."

"How do you mean?"

"That's all I'm saying, mate. All I know is that he was involved down that club and ended up in the canal."

"The poor sod was only sixteen," Said Erin

"In what way was he working at the Havana?"

Mattie looked like he was about to start crying and it was Erin that took over. "Didn't you know? It's one of Croxley's best-kept secrets. They take young girls and boys from the estates and use them as sex toys. I don't know what happened, but obviously, something went wrong, and Jason ended up dead. He was found in the canal, but we know where he went that night and it wasn't fishing. If you're looking for a link, then you should find out what goes on upstairs at the Havana."

"What have the four lad's that were killed got to do with the Havana?"

Mattie lit a cigarette, and I could see that his hand was shaking uncontrollably. "You're the detective, work it out. Boy get's killed by some toff in a club; his brother threatens to go to the police, and then gets beaten up and left for dead. It don't take no fucking genius to see what the link is."

I nodded. "So what you are saying, Mattie; is that they all work for the same person. Am I right?"

"You could be," said Mattie slyly.

"But why would that person be afraid of you going to the police, Mattie?"

"I've not always been a cripple, mate. It could be that I used to work for that person as well, and might have known too much."

"That still doesn't tell me who the person is."

They looked at each other, and I noticed just the slightest nod from Erin.

"You got any more of those twenties?"

I reached into my pocket, brought out some more and laid them on the table. Just like before, he counted them carefully and put them into the pocket of his jeans.

"Well?"

"If you're looking for a name, you should try Charlie Keller for starters. Now if you don't mind, we've got a coach to catch."

CHAPTER SEVENTEEN

"Charlie Keller; now there's a flash from the past; I thought he was legit now."

I had just bought a round of drinks and me and Shoddy were having yet another business meeting in The Hundred.

"So you know him do you, Shod?" I said, turning off the television in the snug and sitting down in my favourite chair.

"Know him, tried to nick him and never came close. The man was bullet proof 20 years ago, so these days he must be untouchable."

"How do you mean bulletproof?"

"He had the right connections and an army of workers who were like little ants running around doing his dirty work. You name it, Moggs, and Keller was making money doing it. He was into drugs, prostitution, protection rackets and even armed robbery. He had money to burn and lined the pockets of the right people, which included the police. Either people were afraid to go near him, or they were on a nice little earner so wanted to protect their income."

"So why did you say that you thought he was legit now?"

"That's the way they all go in the end. I've seen his name a few times in the local paper at charity fundraisers, and I know that even back then he invested heavily in property, both in Britain and abroad. The new leisure centre in town was constructed by his building firm, and I know for a fact that his company does a lot of road works and council house maintenance."

"He sounds like a bad lad."

"You don't mess with Keller and walk away still breathing. If he is the link in all this, then I would stay well clear and let that Tommy character end up in the morgue. Even if you could get to Keller, which is doubtful, you would have to destroy his whole organisation and kill him to have any chance of survival. How much are you getting paid?"

I looked at the empty glasses. "Not enough to risk my neck for Tommy Brand. Another pint, Shod?" I don't know why I bother asking really. He handed me his glass.

"While you're up, get some whisky chasers with those pints, so you don't have to go to the bar again. I've got some things to tell you when you get back."

He waited for me to bring the glasses over to the table and settle back into my seat. I sat back while he rolled a cigarette and got comfortable. He had obviously picked up some information down with his mates at the police station, and it would probably mean more legwork for me.

"So I went down to see the lads at the office."

Shoddy always called the police station where he used to work, the office.

"And?"

He took a swig of beer and then drained his glass of whiskey. "Didn't I say doubles?"

"We haven't got the money for doubles, will you spit out what you have got?"

"Do you remember the brother of Webster? The one that they found floating in the canal?"

"Yes I do, mate. His name was Jerry, no Jason........."

"Yeah, that's the one. Well, apparently he was a crackhead and not against getting some arse action to fund his habit, off anybody who would pay him. Apparently he wasn't fussy and got nicked a few times for illegal soliciting for punters in cars."

"So what's the connection?"

"According to one of the lads, the Havana may not be as clean as people think. There are a few whispers going around about underage shagging going on, but nothing has been proved. Maybe Jason Webster was part of some high-powered sex ring at the Havana. An interesting fact, though, is that the owner of the club is none other than Councillor Gary Evans. Isn't that the bloke you were following for Tommy, so he could write an exposé blockbuster on town hall corruption in Croxley?"

"It was more about his sexual activities though maybe one links with the other. So Evans owns the Havana? I think it's time to have a word."

"He's not going to talk to you, Moggs; unless.............................."

"Unless what?"

"Unless you tell him that you are a reporter. Maybe he will talk to you then."

"If that's the case, maybe Tommy could do it; after all, he actually is a reporter so would know what questions to ask."

"It could all be legal, like any gentleman's club."

"Yeah, and Bill doesn't water down the beer. You've got to be kidding me, Shod. Evans is as bent as they come. I wouldn't put it past him running a brothel, but I still can't see what the connection is with the four lads, or why anybody would want to kill those three men."

Shoddy drained his pint and looked at me expectantly with the empty glass in his hand. "There is something else," he said. "Those fake tits; I got an address of where they were bought. There is only one shop in the whole of Merseyside that does that type of body suit."

"That does surprise me," I said sarcastically.

"No, really, Moggs. They are very expensive and highly specialist; you should go and take a look."

"A false tit shop; I'm really scraping the barrel here, Shod. Didn't the police find out anything there?

"If they did, then nobody is saying. I expect it was DCI Jenkins and Harrison that went there, and they are playing it close to their chests. It's worth a try. Maybe you could offer some money for information. I thought you told me that Tommy has given you a budget."

"I never said that, but he did say I could spend some cash if I needed to."

"Well, spend some friggin cash, mate, and get the beer in. And this time, make those whiskies doubles, you tight git."

CHAPTER EIGHTEEN

TransTorso is the sort of establishment that you would expect to be found up some dark alleyway away from places where normal people do their shopping. When I parked the car in a pay-and-display car park just off Bold Street in Liverpool, I knew from my A to Z that it was only a five-minute walk away. What I hadn't calculated was the rain, and by the time I arrived outside the grubby little entrance with beige blinds over the windows I was soaked. The irony that I was wearing a grey raincoat, and entering a sex shop up an alleyway, wasn't wasted on me though I wasn't laughing out loud.

Inside it was dimly lit, and as you would expect, jammed packed with false breast torsos of every size and colour. I had to admit that if I was ever in the market to buy such an item, then this would certainly be a good place to come. I went over to the counter, which had a load of wigs and false penises, again of every colour and size. Who the hell buys these things?

A figure appeared from behind a curtain at the other end of the room. "Are we interested in a full torso or just a pair of silicones that you stick on with special tapes, sir?"

Shit! It was a woman and a very attractive one at that. "We are no interested in buying anything, Luv. I am looking for some information."

"Really? How intriguing. You must tell me more."

Her soft voice had gone about two tones deeper, and when she came fully into view, I realised that she was in fact, a man. I think it was the stubble that gave her away, but fair do's; from a distance, she looked realistic. I waited for her to move to the other side of the counter.

She had violet eyes and long blonde hair that was obviously a wig but very realistic. "If it's directions that you want, then I'm not from around here, so I would suggest that you go and find a nice jolly policeman.

"No, it's not directions I'm after. I was looking for information about a false silicon breast suit that was sold to someone who used it when murdering three men."

"Ah......so you're from the police?"

"No, I'm working for a journalist, who is writing an article on the murders." She didn't look convinced, so I added, "I'm a private investigator. Here's my card." I gave her my identity card and unlike most people she read it all before giving it back.

"We sell a lot of those specialist suits; they are a fairly newish range."

"So there are different kinds?"

"You would be surprised. We sell upper body shaping, natural silicon hanging breasts, classic curved boobs with and without peephole bras, silicon breast bras and self-adhesive tits in all cup sizes. Plus, we have a special offer on at the moment. The complete beginner makeover set with a wig, upper and lower body suit and for you, I will throw in an extra large false cock, for free. Have I whetted your appetite, sir? Shall I go on?

"No, you're ok."

She smiled at me seductively and looked me up and down. "Anything else whet?"

I ignored the remark. "So you know the type of suit that I'm talking about. The police must have shown it to you."

"They showed me a picture, and I recognised it straight away."

"So what did you tell them about it?"

"Why nothing of course."
"So you don't know who you sold it to?"

"I didn't say that sweetie, what I said was that I didn't tell the police. I've got exactly the same suit on at the moment." She began unbuttoning her dress. "Do you want to see it?"

"Er............no I'm fine thank you. I don't actually need to see the suit I just wanted to know who bought one."

She looked disappointed and began to button herself back up. She picked up a long pole with a hook on it, ran it along a rack above my head and brought down a false body with a huge pair of breasts.

"You get more effect by seeing it on. They can be quite stunning and very sexy."

"I've no doubt about that. But are you saying that you couldn't remember who you sold it to."

"No, what I am saying is that I didn't tell the police anything because I have had enough trouble off them in the past, so I don't owe them anything."

"So?"

"A man with a limp and a scar down his face came in and bought it about a month ago."

"I see. How tall was he?"

"Gosh, you are gullible for a policeman aren't you, sweetness."

"That's private detective, Miss, and are you going to tell me who you sold it to or just keep pissing me around."

She turned around, disappeared into the back of the shop and came back a few minutes later with a piece of paper, which she gave to me. "We have only sold one of those suits in the past year. They are too expensive. Most people go for the cheaper stick on jobbies."

"What do I owe you?" I asked getting out my wallet.

"This one's on me love, just get the bastard who did it will you, for me."

"Why? Did you know the men involved?"

"No, those bastards more than likely deserved it. I just don't like people misusing our products."

The address that was written down that she had given me was in Walton, and I joined the late afternoon commuter traffic on the A5057 and began the slow crawl past endless roadworks. After about a half an hour drive I turned off onto the A59 that took me near Goodison Park, which is the home of Everton Football Club. This is the team my dad used to drag me to see when I was a kid. I tuned in the local radio to see if there had been any development on the murders, and was surprised to find none other than Councillor Evans being interviewed. He sounded very sincere, and I settled back to listen to what he had to say as I waited for yet another traffic light to turn green

Evans had a very sombre tone to his voice when he spoke. "I knew all of the men that were killed, and I have to say that there were no harder working members of the town council than Cyril Blackmore and William Jones. Both were solid pillars of the community and loving family men. They will be sorely missed.

"Did you know Superintendant Blake, Mr Evans?" Said the female interviewer.

"I knew Joe when he was just your average constable on the beat in Liverpool; only there was nothing average about him. He was a wonderful man, and the local community where he lived with his wife Jill, are still reeling under the shock. He was so active in his spare time and did a lot of good work for charity."

"So are the police any nearer to finding out who it is that is committing these heinous murders?"

"The police are working very hard and have a few leads, which they are following up. It is tough work and a slow process, but I believe in law and order, and I know that the perpetrator of all of these scurrilous attacks will be caught."

"So let's turn to you now, Councillor Evans. Tell me what plans have you got to ensure that the people of Croxley are safe from attack."

"I think that you can see already that there are more police on the streets of Croxley, and there are a spot checks on motorists on all roads going in and out of the town. Of course, you can never have enough resources, and my advice to everybody is to keep alert."

"But do you think that there is any connection with the three men killed at the Havana Club, and the four in Stanley Street?"

"Now that's the million dollar question, Jenny. There does not seem to be any connection between the victims....."

"They were all male..."

"Yes, they were male, and all had a connection with Croxley, but apart from this, there is nothing obvious.

"What about organised crime you, jerk?" I shouted at the radio. "Oh yes, and ask him who owns the Havana Club." I'd had enough and was almost at my destination, so I aborted the good councillor and switched him, and the brainless bimbo interviewing him, off.

I turned into Black Diamond Terrace and cruised down it looking for number 28. It was a long street, and the houses were mainly semi-detached and terrace. The distinguishing feature that made the one I was looking for stand out from the rest was that it had been burnt down, and was now just a pile of rubble. I got out of my car and walked down the path towards the front door, which was just a gap in the wall. I wondered if it was safe to go through, and if it was worth the trouble.

"Are you from the Insurance Company?" I turned and saw a woman watching me from across the street. She was dressed in a tweed coat and hat and carrying a Tesco Shopping Bag. The bits of flesh I could see of her looked old. I made my way over in the hope that she liked to gossip.

"Yes, I am. How did you guess?"

"You get to know instinctively what people do for a living when you get to my age, Luv. Not many people wear a suit and trilby around here, and you don't look as if you are selling double glazing. She looked at my dilapidated Riley Elf and gave me a quizzical look that demanded an answer.

I looked my car up and down and shrugged. "I didn't want to bring the Rover to this area. I'm not being funny, but it might get vandalised, or stolen by those gangs you're always hearing about on the radio. This is my wife's run-around."

She nodded wisely. "Yeah, the kids are little terrors around here. I don't blame you."

I tried to focus her mind on the burnt-out house. "So can you tell me what happened over there, luv?"

"What? You mean the house? Well before it was burnt down it was full of them travellers and gypsies. You know the type I mean; them sort that don't do nothing all day and smoke those drug things at night."

"So it was occupied then?"

"I don't think that they were paying any rent. If you ask me, I think that they were squatting."

"So who owned the house?"

Another quizzical look. "Don't you know? Isn't the name on the policy?"

"Er........Yeah, that's right, but I just have to check." I touched my nose conspiratorially, and her face brightened.

"We never saw the people who owned it. The place was always filled up with scum of one sort or the other. Course, we all knew that it would end badly, and when it caught fire, nobody in the street was surprised."

"Tell me about what happened." I got my notebook and pencil out to look more official.

"It was two weeks on Sunday.........no, hang on a minute, it was a Monday because I remember that I had just taken the washing in, and Monday is washing day around here."

"So tell me in your own words."

"Well, everybody just does the washing on a Monday; it's sort of traditional............"

"Sorry, I didn't mean tell me about the washing, I meant the fire."

"Oh, that. The fire happened about eight o'clock in the evening. There was a loud explosion, and everybody came running out into the street. It was like bonfire night. I ain't seen nothing like it since the Germans were bombing us. The fire brigade arrived pretty quickly because the station is only around the corner, but by this time, all of the people from the house had gone."

"Gone?"

"Yes, Luv; gone. They all disappeared into the night to find some other derelict property to destroy and good riddance I say. They were bringing the area down, with people going in and out at all times of the night, and the dogs barking. Yes, and the smell of some of them. They must not have had any washing facilities to have a bath."

"Can you remember if a post van delivered a parcel to the address sometime before the incident happened?"

She frowned and shook her head. "Why do you ask?"

I lowered my voice, moved closer and leaned down into her face. "It could have been a bomb."

She looked startled, and I handed her my card. "If you ask some of your neighbours if any of them saw a parcel being delivered, I would be grateful if you could give me a ring."

She looked at the card and mouthed the words Morris Shannon Private Investigator. That seem to satisfy her, and she told me she would do that for me. I watched her carry the shopping into a small terraced house on the other side of the road, and I went back into the garden and through the gap in the wall, hoping that the wall would not fall down on me.

There was not a lot to see, just a pile old smoke damaged bricks and charred wood. I turned around to go back through the opening, and I saw it. On the inner part of the front wall, was a huge drawing in black paint of a hangman figure with two legs, but no arms.

CHAPTER NINETEEN

"So have you had any luck deciphering the message under the hangman yet?" Said Tommy.

I was sitting in Shoddy's flat eating breakfast when the phone had rung. I had spent the last 20 minutes going through what I had been doing the day before, and he kept stopping me and asking questions. It sounded like he was writing it all down on the other side of the line and I wasn't impressed. In the morning, I was never at my best before I had eaten and had a drink, and now my eggs and bacon were congealed and my coffee untouched and cold.

"No, Tommy, I have not had any luck working out the frigging letters because I have been running around like a headless chicken. Besides, you never even used the information about the hangman card in your column. Did you forget?"

"It's all part of the master plan, Moggsy. Why use a piece of information so valuable at this stage? I want that interview with the Dark Angel, and then I will reveal everything."

"Unless somebody beats you to it."

"Don't worry about me, Moggsy. I'm a master at this, and I know when to give out information and when to keep schtum."

"Well I'm sure that you know what you're doing, mate: is that all you wanted?"

"No, there was another thing. I've got you an interview with Councillor Gareth Evans, this afternoon at three at the town hall."

"What? Why did you do that?"

"Easy, Moggs; I just told his secretary that I was from the national press and was interested in asking a few questions about keeping everybody safe in Croxley."

"So we're going together, then?"

"No, I think that it's best that you go and talk to the old rogue. Give him the usual spiel about being a private investigator working for a journalist. Tell him you want to talk about the human element of the murders."

"I don't feel very happy about this, Tommy."

"You are going to be alright, just ask him about his connection with the Havana, and also about all the work that Charlie Keller's company is getting from the council, like building the new swimming pool."

"I didn't know that. How did you find out?"

"I did a bit of digging on my own. It is very interesting if you start looking in the right places. Keller Construction does a lot of contract work from the council. Most of the jobs have been bid for against other local companies, and it seems that Keller Construction always comes out on top."

"Wouldn't it be better, seeing as you know all about it, that you come as well?"

"If I went, then what would be the point of you coming Moggsy? Besides, I am phoning you from London. I have a few meetings with some newspapers, and I won't be back until late tonight. Don't forget, Moggs, the town hall at three. Oh and Moggsy."

"Yeah?"

"Wear something decent." With that, the cheeky bastard put the phone down on me.

Shoddy was re-frying the bacon and eggs, and when I sat back down at the table, he placed a mug of steaming coffee in front of me.

"I've added some fried bread," he said, returning to the stove and flipping the egg over. "That Tommy can go on; he could talk internationally for England. I wouldn't like to be paying his telephone bill. I still don't see why he hasn't mentioned the hangman card left on the bodies. If he doesn't watch out, somebody else will get the information, and he will be kicking himself." He walked over and placed my breakfast in front of me for the second time. The egg looked a strange colour after spending so much time in the frying pan.

"That's what I said to him, but he says it's all part of the master plan."

Shoddy went over to the easel that he had set up in the middle of the room. He wrote the random letters down, studied them, and then drew the picture of the hangman. There are two arms to go, so my guess is that we are going to see another two murder scenes."

"But why the hangman and the letters, Shod?"

"Deranged mind? A hidden message? I haven't got a clue, and neither have the police. He began to write down bullet points and join them up with lines. He wrote Keller's name at the top.

"Keller is the connection here. He used those scallies to beat up Mathew Webster. Jason Webster could have a possible link with the Havana Club. But how does this link up with Keller?"

"What about Evans? He is the owner of the Havana Club, and from what Tommy is saying, could well be getting money off Keller for giving him building contracts. Maybe it goes deeper than that. Maybe Keller and Evans are partners."

"I think that we're clutching at straws here. You've got more chance of playing centre forward for Liverpool than finding out who this killer is, and setting up an appointment with Tommy." He looked at his watch. "Anyway the pubs are open, so let's go and have a few beers and mull it all over."

"I've got an interview with Evans this afternoon, and I can't turn up smelling of booze."

"Then it looks like we're on the vodkas, doesn't it, soft lad."

You couldn't argue with his logic. I grabbed my coat and followed him out the door. I had to admit; the guy could move when he wanted to.

CHAPTER TWENTY

I arrived ten minutes early at the town hall. I gave the receptionist my name, and she showed me into a waiting room and said that Councillor Evans would be with me in just a minute. The room gave off about as much ambience as toxic waste, and the green institutional paint job on the walls reminded me of Croxley police station's number two interview room, which I was well acquainted with.

There were no magazines on the glass coffee table in the centre of the room, and no window to look out of, so I prepared myself to be bored for at least the next half hour. That's what these type of people do isn't it? Play power games with time. I decided to keep myself amused by going over the case, but I needn't have bothered because in less than a minute the same receptionist came back, and said those magical words. "Councillor Evans will see you now, Mr Shannon.

The room Evans was sitting in was like something out of a book by Charles Dickens, and as I sat across an ornate oak desk looking at him, I felt like I had stepped back into the 17th century.

"And you say that you are not a reporter for a national newspaper, Mr ....er...Shannon," he said examining my business card closely for the second time. He was dressed in a brilliant white shirt with the sleeves rolled up and a blue silk tie unbuttoned to make him look hard working.

"That's right, but my associate, Mr Thomas Brand is in London and couldn't be here." He examined me like a cat would examine a mouse before killing it, and run his bony fingers through his thin grey hair. I pulled out my notebook and pencil and gave him my best innocent smile.

"Mr Brand will be writing our interview, or parts of it, when I give him my notes later this evening."

"Well this is most irregular, Mr Shannon; most irregular indeed. I have a meeting coming up soon, so you will need to be quick." He played with my card, examined it one more time and put it into the drawer of his desk.

"So what are your thoughts about the murders, Councillor Evans?"

He leaned back in his chair and put his hands behind his head. "I feel the same as everybody else in Croxley. I have Sympathy for the families of the people that were killed and shocked by the manner of the deaths."

"Is there any indication from the police that they are close to finding out who the identity of the murderer is?"

"At this stage, the police are playing things very close to their chest." He smiled conspiratorially. "Even someone in my position is not in the investigation loop, though; I do suspect that they have some strong ideas about the type of person they are looking for."

"And what sort of a person would that be?"

"Well, your guess is as good as mine, but I would say that we are dealing with a mind that is completely distorted. I feel that whoever could do such terrible things to another human being is very sick and needs to be taken out from society and locked up."

"So would you advocate hanging the person?"

"A person that could do crimes such as these does not deserve to live, but I respect the fact that we have chosen to abolish the death sentence. I do, however, think, Mr Shannon, that our society has gone too soft on wrongdoers and members of organised crime gangs."

"So, are you saying that organised crime in Croxley is out of control?"

"What I am saying is that the person who murdered those seven people is out of control."

"So you believe that there is no organised crime in Croxley."

"I think the police are doing an excellent job in Croxley with very little resources."

"But you think that organised crime in Croxley is not a problem?"

"I'm not sure what organised crime has got to do with the seven murders, Mr Shannon."

"According to my investigations, there could be a link between one particular criminal organisation that operates in and around the Croxley area and the reason for the murders. I am including in this, the Havana Club."

"I'm sorry, Mr Shannon, but I'm a counsellor not a law enforcement officer, so I have little knowledge about gang warfare in the Croxley area."

"But you are the owner of the Havana Club."

This made him sit up and take his hands from behind his head. He narrowed his grey-green eyes at me. "I have an interest in the Havana club, but this is legal and above board for everyone to see."

"Are you acquainted with Keller Construction and the company's successful bid last month to build the new swimming pool in town?"

He looked at his watch and smiled coldly. "I'm sorry, Mr Shannon, but I have got another appointment in five minutes." He got up and held his hand out.

"Are you aware that the owner of Keller construction is a well known local criminal, with interests that include prostitution, drugs, protection rackets and armed robbery?"

The door opened, and the receptionist reappeared. The bastard must have pressed some hidden button to call her. His hand dropped to his side though the smile remained fixed on his face.

"I think that these are questions you should ask somebody from the police, Mr Shannon. Miss Bowden, will you show, Mr Shannon out, please. With that, he sat down and picked up the telephone. Meeting over!

When I got back to the office, I gave Tommy a call and told him what had happened. I was still annoyed that he hadn't come with me though now I knew the reason.

"You're a sly bastard, Tommy."
"Oh yeah? What do you mean by that?"

"You frigging knew that Evans was going to go ape-shit when I asked him about his interests in the Havana Club and Keller Construction."

"Why? What did he say?"

"He practically threw me out. I don't think I made a new friend there. He didn't even give me a straight answer to any of my questions. You should have come with me, Tommy."

"I wish I could have, but I was putting the finishing touches to a deal that is going to make us both a lot of money."

"What sort of a deal?"

"The sort of a deal where you are going to have to start doing your job, and get me an interview with the Dark Angel. If we can pull this off, Moggsy, we have cracked it. It will not only get national interest, but I can get us space in papers all over the world."

"Oh, that. I'm no closer to finding out who the evil bastard is than I was a week ago. Let's face it, Tommy, it could be anybody, and I've used up all of the leads that I have been following."

There was silence on the other end of the phone as if Tommy was thinking. Finally, he said. "I can keep it all bubbling along nicely, with some stuff about Evans and how he may be involved in some way."

"What? You are not going to say that he is a suspect are you? If you do that, he's going to come after me with a solicitor. Can't you write about something else?"

"That's not how it works, Moggsy. Just leave it to me. I'll do the writing, and you do the investigating. Now, what have you got lined up?"

"Well, I was thinking about driving over to the pub, having a few beers and then going to bed."

"You're hardly prolific are you, Moggsy? Don't forget; I've paid you for this. I will give you a call tomorrow, and I will expect you to have something for me to write about.

I was going to tell him where to shove his money, but as I had already spent most of it, decided on a bit of discretion. "Yeah, ok Tommy, I'll see what I can do."

He put the phone down on me, and I got a can of beer out of the drawer in my desk and tried to come up with some possible leads that I could investigate. After five minutes I still hadn't written anything, so I got my hat and coat and headed for the door. It was eight o'clock, raining and I needed a drink. I had parked my car in the alley at the side of the betting shop, underneath my office. My Riley Elf was behind the bins, and I prayed that she was going to start.

As I was walking towards it, I heard footsteps behind me, which echoed off the wet cobblestones. I turned around instinctively and saw two men coming towards me. I couldn't make out much detail, except that they were big and looked like trouble.

"Mr Shannon?"

Here we go! I turned fully to face them and saw that at least one was carrying a very big knife. "Who wants to know?" I tried to sound brave but didn't think I succeeded. At the very least I was just going to get a kicking, but I dreaded to think what the worst-case scenario was going to be.

The two men separated, and the one with the knife came towards me threateningly. "You've been making a bit of a nuisance of yourself with the wrong person, Shannon. It looks like you need a lesson in manners." He held the knife out, and I backed away getting ready to make a run for it. I was expecting the first man to rush me and tried to remember my knife self-defense skills. Let him come at you, turn to the side, trap the hand holding the knife with your left hand and karate chop his neck with the right; or was it the other way around? As it was, I never found out, which was correct. Instead of rushing me, he stopped dead in his tracks and fell to his knees as if he was going to pray. The other man started backing away, and then the lights went out in my world.

CHAPTER TWENTY-ONE

It was probably the rain that brought me around. I opened my eyes, and even though my vision was blurred, I could see that I was still in the alleyway. Somebody had propped up against the wall. It all came flooding back into my head like mental diarrhoea, and I shot to my feet and had to hold onto one of the bins to stop myself passing out.

The man that had been about to attack me was lying on his back with his eyes wide open staring lifelessly at the sky. The other one was there too, in a similar position only without his head. That was propped up on the top of the bin I was leaning on with a hangman card nailed to the forehead. The little figure now had two legs and one arm, which I noted, before vomiting in disgust. I had to get to the car and get away as quickly as I could. If I was found near another one of the murders, it wasn't going to look good. I rushed into the Elf and fired her up, but before moving off realised that I had forgotten something important. I fished in my pocket for my pencil and notepad and went back to the severed head.

I wrote down very carefully the letters; and as I had suspected, there were more of them. The sequence now read:

N _ T H _ _ _   P _ _ S _ N A _

I got back into the Elf and drove away.

It was late afternoon the next day before I finally got to hear about what had happened in the alley. I was waiting in The Hundred while Shoddy had gone to the police station to see what the crime scene boys had picked up about the murders. By the time he arrived back it, it was almost six o'clock. I patiently waited while he bought himself a drink and joined me in the snug. He drained half of it, wiped his mouth, then went through his irritating ritual of rolling a cigarette before speaking.

"The two lads that were killed were not from around here, so they couldn't be connected to any criminal gang in Croxley. They both had form though and had done time for GBH and minor stuff that mostly revolved around violence. Nobody down the station has a clue what they were doing down an alley, but they are starting a house to house search to see if they can dig anything up. As your office is next door to the alley, I think it is safe to say that you are going to get a call, so we had better work out a story."

"We both know who is behind this, Shod."

"Evans you mean?"

"It has to be him, mate. It's just too much of a coincidence that I go and ask him some difficult questions, and the next thing that happens is two gorillas are threatening me."

"Looks like this Dark Angel character, saved your life, Moggs."

"Yeah, it looks that way. I guess I owe her a pint."

"She would probably thank you more for a Bloody Mary, Moggs."

"Yeah, she certainly is a gruesome bitch. I wouldn't want to get on the wrong side of her. So how did she kill them?"

"As always, she was quite ingenious. They were both paralyzed with small darts that had been dipped in curare."

"What's curare?"

"It's used by South American tribesmen to hunt animals. They use blowpipes and it paralysis the prey, so it can't move."

"So in this instance, it paralysed those two scumbags. Then what?"

One of them was knifed in the heart while he was still alive, and the other had his head removed, probably by using a saw because of the jagged way the neck was cut."

"Phew, Shod. How come she left me alone?

"Well, if you think about it, this is the second time she could have killed you but hasn't. Maybe she fancies you, mate.

"Yep," I said draining my glass. I picked up Shoddy's and made my way to the bar.

When I was at the bar waiting to be served somebody tapped me on my shoulder and I swung round getting ready to hit them. I was still on edge from what had happened in the alley.

"Steady on, Shannon; I didn't come here for a fight though it looks like most of the other people in here did. When you told me your local was rough, you weren't exaggerating were you?" It was Tommy standing behind me, looking out of place in his three-piece pinstripe suit and black Crombie. He was already getting some strange looks off some of the boys in the bar, so I steered him into the seclusion of the snug and sat him down next to Shoddy.

"What do you want to drink Tommy? And don't ask for a gin and tonic because the landlord Bill would think you're a shirt lifter."

"I'll have a pint of snakebite, if you're buying, Morris."

Shoddy looked impressed with his choice. "Yeah, get me one of those as well, Moggs, I haven't had snakebite in years."

"I'll get it if you explain what the Hell it is. You know how confused Bill gets if you don't order either lager or whiskey."

"It's best bitter with cider in equal portions."

"Don't I know you?" said Shoddy, looking Tommy up and down."

"I don't think I've had the pleasure," said Tommy holding out his hand.

When I got back, I found them deep in conversation about the Dark Angel and trying to work out what the two words were underneath the hangman. By the time the last orders bell rang, they still hadn't come up with a reasonable combination, but both agreed that it was some kind of foreign name.

Shoddy was convinced it was NATHANI PANSINAL, which he insisted was of Indian or Pakistani origin. When pressed, as we made our way home eating fish and chips, he admitted that it was probably the drink talking and that he still didn't have a clue. I had filled in the details of my experience in the alleyway to Tommy, and he refused our offer of chips, as he said he had to get back to write up the article for the newspaper the next day.

Shoddy was still insisting that he knew him, but I suspected that this was the drink talking too. As always when Shoddy was worse for wear due to drink I listened but didn't take much notice of what he said. As I was going through the door on my way to bed, he reached into his pocket and passed me a piece of paper.

"Oh yeah, I almost forgot. I got this name when I was with some of the lads down the station."

On the paper was the name Dillon Richard, with an address." What's this, mate?"

"I know that you didn't get much information out of Mathew Webster about his brother, but Dillon Richard was Jason's best friend in more ways than one if you know what I mean."

"Thanks, Shod, it's worth a try. I'll go and see him tomorrow."

When I got back to my flat, I went through my usual ritual of taking a beer, sitting on my balcony and listening to the distant rumble of the motorway. It was raining, which was the weather that best fitted my mood. If nothing came out of the meeting with Jason's friend I had pretty much decided to jack the case in and wait for another one to turn up. Being almost beaten up by those goons in the alleyway had partially made up my mind for me. To get involved in life threatening situations again, I was going to need to be paid a lot more than Tommy Brand had any intention of giving me. Call me, plain old Mr Boring, but even if my life wasn't that great, it was something that I didn't want to give up just yet. I fell asleep with that thought in my head and stumbled into bed in the early hours of the morning. I could still hear Shoddy moving around next door, as I turned the bedside table light off, and pulled the pillow over my head.

CHAPTER TWENTY-TWO

The old industrial estate off the A362 heading for Bootle doesn't exist anymore though the names of the streets were kept out of respect for the areas heritage. In a spot where a famous household name sugar company used to have its refinery sit three luxurious detached houses. One of the houses is owned by semi-famous Liverpool Rock Star who made his money in the 1960s and now tours the social club circuit and hopes one day that he will be able to make a comeback. The second is still empty because nobody can afford the asking price, and the third belongs to Charles Darwin Keller. The middle name of Darwin was his mother's idea and was the cause of many a fight in the school playground as boys would be boys and took the piss. Keller grew up the hard way in Birkenhead and learnt in junior school that money came easily if you terrorised your fellow pupils. The fact that he enjoyed inflicting pain was a bonus, and by the time he was 12 he had already set up his own drugs business, selling marijuana and Purple Hearts for a local gang of villains.

By the time he was 16, he had got rid of the gang leaders and was running the show himself not only in Birkenhead but also in Liverpool. He had no preference for any particular illegal activity and drugs, teenage prostitution, extortion, armed robbery and murder were all areas that he excelled in. He had no friends and had never had a serious relationship with a woman. He was a cold-blooded killer when it came to his enemies. Many had stood up to him as he was building his crime empire, and many ended up in the Mersey chained to concrete, or in the foundations of motorways.

Now, Keller was at the top of the heap and had connections all over Merseyside both legitimate and illegal. He controlled everything from his luxury Mock-Tudor mansion. He lived here alone though he did have lots of sex with both girls and boys, as child sex was a particular habit he had acquired along his journey to the top. These kids never lasted long, and if they were lucky and didn't upset him, they were allowed to leave and carry on their lives. The unlucky ones ended up dead; killed for amusement purposes only. At his level of power, he had complete control over the environment he lived in and ruled all aspects of his business and private life, with the same ease that he controlled the temperature of his Jacuzzi.

For his age, Keller is in tip-top condition. He had a gym built in the house and works every day with his own personal trainer. Up until a couple of weeks ago, everything in his world was almost perfect, but now all of that had changed, and it was all because of the Dark Angel. Ever since she had killed four of his drug dealers, everybody was running scared in his organisation that they would be next on the list. Keller had seen off many an attempt to take control of his organisation before but they were never like this. The final straw was having two of his best hit men brutally murdered. It had sent a shockwave through his organisation, and even on the legal side of his business, people like Evans from the town council were getting scared. People that were scared could be dangerous as they were unpredictable. He may have to do something about Evans before he did something stupid.

Keller knew that in the business he was in, if there was the slightest hint that he was not in control anymore, then the sharks would start circling getting ready to attack. If it was believed, even by one of those wankers on the streets outside pubs selling his drugs, that he was not in control, then things would start to crumble. It needed to be stamped out and as soon as possible. He was sure that whoever it was that was doing the killing was trying to destroy him, but he didn't know why or who had sent the bitch. It could be a rival mob from Manchester, or even the Chinese, who would have loved to be taking just half of the money that he was out of protection and extortion. There had always been an unspoken rule between him and the triads that they would leave each other alone. He dismissed the idea. This was not their style of doing business. With them, it was all out war, not stealth. This had to be something that he had missed. In his life, he had made a lot of enemies. It must be something to do with this.

His second in command is a small man with cold dark eyes, jet black hair and a swarthy Latin complexion that had learnt over the years how to survive the Keller paranoia. There had been many a cull of bosses in the Keller Empire over the years, and Frank Poole kept his head down and struggled to the position of power that he now held. He has never seen his boss so agitated as he is now, and he knows that he has to tread carefully because any word out of place could mean death.

"I want this bastard alive, Frank, do you hear me? Alive." Keller threw down the newspaper that had a full page on the latest incident involving the Dark Angel and the death of his men.

Pool took a sip of coffee and waited. Part of the survival process that he had learnt was to only speak when he was asked a direct question by his boss and then to be very careful on how that question was answered.

Keller continued his rant. "Anymore of this, and the rats will sense I'm not in control. I want you to find out who she is and bring her to me. I want answers, Frank, and I'm not getting them at the moment. Well? Don't just sit there drinking my fucking coffee, get out and do something. Get me some results and fast, I want an end to all of this. I'm relying on you, Frank; don't fuck-up on this one and I will make it worth your while."

Keller watched Pool disappear through the door and watched through the window as he started up his Mercedes and drove through the electric gates. Down below in the garden, a couple of figures came out of the shadows with walkie-talkies and watched as the Mercedes disappeared into the distance, then checked that the gates had closed properly. Keller knew that at least in his house, nobody could get to him. He had a handpicked team of security staff and some of the best surveillance equipment that money could buy.

Maybe that's why she was attacking the people he employed and his associates. She knew that he was so well protected that she couldn't get to him personally, so she was trying to destroy all of the hard work he had done and the years of building. She was doing a good job so far, but it had to be stopped.

That fucking murdering bitch was dead meat. He trusted Frank Poole as much as he had trusted anyone in his life, and if anybody could find out who this person was, it was him. He just hoped that before she was killed, he could torture the truth out of her, and resolve the questions that had been keeping him awake at night. Why was she trying to destroy him, and who had sent her?

CHAPTER TWENTY-THREE

"It's coming up to 9 o'clock on a cold and wet Monday here on radio Croxley, and we're here with Councillor Gareth Evans, who has very kindly come in to talk about the Dark Angel. Councillor, you said earlier that we should all be on our guard and look for anything suspicious. Does this mean that we are all at risk?"

"I think, Suzy, that whoever has carried out these murders has a deranged mind and is just hitting out at anyone who is unlucky enough to be in the wrong place at the wrong time."

"So in your opinion, there are no links between the people who have been killed."

"Absolutely. I think that you would be hard pressed to find anything that links the four boys killed in Stanley Street to the two men recently murdered. And of course, we have two councillors and a high ranking police superintendent killed at the Havana club. You would have to have a very vivid imagination to find any common link between the three incidents."

"But haven't some of the newspapers said that for instance, the last two people killed, could have been local criminals?"

"That is absolute rubbish, Suzy. This is just sensationalism on the part of journalists, who are trying to take this story and make it into something that it's not. The police have not released any information that these men were anything more than people going about their normal business. Are they also saying the three dignitaries killed at the Havana were criminals as well?

"So according to you, these have been random killings, and everyone is at risk."

"Exactly. Until we know the truth, this is all that we can assume. There is no logic to what this so-called Dark Angel is doing, and the newspapers should be ashamed of themselves for giving her a motive. The victims were not bad people as some of the journalists are trying to make us believe. They were just in the wrong place at the wrong time and will be sadly missed by their loved ones..............."

I leaned over switched off the radio and finished off my mug of tea; I'd had enough of Councillor Evans and his bullshit.

"I tell you what, Shod; I hope it's that bastard who is next on the list. Getting his head sawn off is too good for him. How he can go on the radio and lie like that is beyond me."

"He's a politician ain't he; they all lie and never give anyone a straight answer. I would be more surprised if Evans started telling the truth."

"The thing is, Shod, no matter what he says, we are still no closer to finding out the identity of the Dark Angel, and it looks as if we never will.

Shoddy shrugged. "So how much do you know about Tommy?"

"Not a lot; why are you still going on about that?"

"It's just that I still think that I know him from somewhere. You know me, Moggs, I never forget a face. And that face of his haunted my dreams last night."

"To be honest, we don't know very much about him. I don't even know where he lives when he is in Croxley. Why do you think it's so important? As long as he keeps the money flowing it's OK by me."

He got up, took the mugs over to the sink and ran some hot water into them. "It's nothing really, but I'm going to pop down the station to see the lads later on. I've got a hunch that the last time I saw that face, was when I was a police constable."

"So you're saying that Tommy is a villain?"

"I don't know what I'm saying at the moment, Moggs; I just want to find out. I think I'll check out where he is living as well, just to make sure."

When I left him, it was just after ten o'clock, and he was opening his first can of cheap cider. If he was starting this early in the morning, I only hoped that he was going to be in a fit state to make it through the door.

I made my way to my car and hoped that my visit to see Dillon Richard wasn't going to be a waste of time.

CHAPTER TWENTY-FOUR

The man behind the counter of the A to Z Video shop looks up as the bell rings to announce new customers are entering. Two hard looking men walk in dressed in jeans, t-shirts and bomber jackets. One of them turns the sign in the window of the door around so that it now displays closed. They hang around the Action & Adventure section browsing through titles waiting for the last person to leave, which is a young boy clutching a copy of Scarface. When they are satisfied that the shop is now empty, they walk nonchalantly over to the counter.

The man behind the counter knows exactly what they want. It is what they come for every week, and he has the brown paper envelope ready for them at the back of the till. He hands it to the tallest of the men, who takes it and rips it open.

"There's no need to count it because it's all there." The shop owner looks alarmed because the men have never done this before.

The man flicks through the used ten and five-pound notes quickly and looks up mockingly at the shop owner. "It's better to be safe than sorry; there are so many rogues around these days that want to rip you off." The two men laugh at this, and then the one holding the money stops laughing and shakes his head.

"This bag is twenty pounds short, pal."

"It's what I always give you," said the shopkeeper sensing trouble.

"The price of protection in this town has just gone up."

"Since when?"

"Since all those people got wasted by that fucking lunatic that's walking around with an axe and a shotgun. It's twenty quid more now." The man held his hand out and gave a sly wink.

The shopkeeper is in a dilemma. He has been paying protection money for about three years, and it has always been the same. Is this young thug trying to get more money for himself, or has the price increase come from people above him?

"Look, pal, you either pay up the money or we take the amount owed out of your head. What's your missus going to say if you come home with no teeth and a broken nose?" The other man took out a leather cosh and slammed it down on the counter. "Or even not come home at all?"

That is enough pressure needed. The shopkeeper goes into the till and gets out four five pound notes and passes them over.

"That's better," said the man holding the bag. He puts the notes inside it and picks up a couple of videos off the counter. "You don't mind if I take these do you?"

The bell sounds above the door, and the two men swivel around to see who has come in. A person wearing a cyclist's helmet with a scarf and goggles hiding the face, saunters leisurely into the shop, carrying a big brown bag.

"Can't you read the fucking writing on the door, pal? We're closed, so fuck off before you get hurt." The man with the cosh raises it menacingly. It doesn't seem to faze the intruder, who throws the bag on the floor and rushes at the two men with what looks like an aerosol canister. Before they have time to react, the content has been squirted in their faces. Whatever it is in the canister has an instant effect. The intruder doesn't even bother looking as they both fall to the floor screaming and clutching their eyes. The effect of sulphuric acid on the skin is devastating, and they aren't going to be causing problems to anybody for the immediate future. The tall man has dropped the brown paper envelope and the two videos.

The shopkeeper gets down behind the counter and waits while the intruder goes to the brown bag on the floor and brings out what looks like a very strange pistol but is in fact, a penetrating cattle stunner. This will imminently be used to send a bolt into the brains of both the men now writhing in agony on the floor. It is over in a matter of seconds; the intruder delicately, almost lovingly, leans over each man in turn and puts him out of his misery. They are now, either dead or if they are unlucky, just brain dead. The figure in the helmet picks up the brown paper package and videos, puts them on the counter, drops a card on one of the bodies and walks out of the shop.

The shopkeeper hears the door bell ring as the intruder leaves. He reaches across the table at the back, picks up the receiver and dials 999 with a hand that he can't stop from shaking. He is then violently sick.

CHAPTER TWENTY-FIVE

The address for Dillon Richard was in the crappy little indoor meat market, which is the beating heart of Croxley's poxy shopping centre. I wasn't expecting him to be a butcher, but I was rather taken aback that the small room, which served as his shop, and was surrounded by stalls selling stuff like lamb chops and pigs heads, was, in fact, a men's hair salon. There was someone with a blood stained apron sitting in the chair when I entered. He was either the lunatic murderer that I was tracking, and my quest was now officially over, or a butcher. The smart money was on the latter, and when he eventually got up and looked at his gleaming short-back-and -sides in the mirror it was confirmed. He pressed loose change into Richard's hand and slapped a plastic bag of sausages down on the top of the till.

Dillon Richard was in his mid-thirties and dressed as you would expect a barber to be dressed, in a white jacket with scissors and a comb sticking out of the top pocket and nondescript black trousers. It was from the shoulders upwards that he seems to be having trouble with his gender settings. His hair was long and ash blonde, and he had heavily made up eyes like a panda and pink lipstick. The broken boxer's nose and facial scarring threw out a warning; backed up by the bulging biceps and neck muscles that this was not a person to mess with.

When he spoke, it was with a strong Salford accent, which was soft and ever so slightly effeminate. "Can I do you now sir?" Now whose was that catch phrase? He held his hand out to show me that the chair was unoccupied.

"I'm not here for a haircut." I took my hat off revealing my bald head. That took the smile off his face but quick as a flash he said: "How about a brush and polish, then?"

I handed him my card, and his stance became ever so slightly more aggressive.

"Oh yeah? Who sent you? If it's money you're after go and pump it out of one of the meat boys because they're loaded with the stuff." He picked up his packet of sausages and stuffed them into a drawer as if he thought I was going to steal them.

"Don't worry, son, your sausages are safe, and nobody has sent me. I'm here for information about a friend of yours, Jason Webster."

"He's dead."

"Yes I know that, but the man who has hired me thinks that his death could be linked to the spate of murders that are happening at the moment."

"You mean the Dark Angel?"

Christ, Tommy was right; it didn't take long for the sheep to start bleating the same contrived name. "Yes, Mr Richard, I'm talking about the Dark Angel incidents."

He seemed to relax a bit more, and reached into his pocket, brought out a Sherlock Holmes shaped pipe, and lit it up. This guy was a psychiatrist's dream ticket. I reckon if you delved deeply into his mind you could get a book out of it.

He sat down behind his desk and offered me the barber's chair. I checked that there were no cut throat razors anywhere near me, just in case he also had Sweeney Todd tendencies.

"So what can I do for you Mr.....................?"

"Shannon. All I want is for you to tell me what connection Jason had with the Havana Club." That got him puffing harder on his pipe. He thought about it without saying anything, and when he spoke, it was as if he was trying to choose his words carefully.

"Most people............er............like Jason and I, did some...............shall we call it, hostess work at the Havana, from time to time. Jason got more than most because he was a good looking boy. He was one of the favourites."

"So, do you think that being a.............hostess had anything to do with his death?"

"You're not from the police, Mr Shannon, so I don't have to tell you fuck all."

"That's right, son, you don't." I waited for him to speak.......................he seemed to be mulling it over. "Common, Dillon; I'm one of the good guys trying to make sense of what is happening here. If you can help, it might stop the next poor bastard from being killed."

"Those poor bastards as you call them, all deserve to be killed."

"Oh yeah, why's that?"

"I'm saying nothing. You want to find out about Jason's death go to the town hall and ask Gareth Evans, you go and talk to those four crack-heads that beat up Jason and threw him into the canal. Oh, just a minute, I forgot. You can't can you because they are all dead. Good riddance I say. I wonder which of these scumbags will be next."

"So why would anybody want to kill Jason if he was as popular as you said he was?"

Dillon shrugged. "I dunno; maybe you should talk to his brother Mattie. Maybe you should ask why a villain like him should go all self-righteous just because it's his brother that's getting bummed by rich old men."

"Mattie has gone, Dillon. No forwarding address. He's done a bunk with his girlfriend and can't be traced."

"Just as well I suppose," muttered Dillon.

"So what you are saying is that Mattie was the reason that his brother got killed."

"What I am saying, Mr Shannon is that Mattie didn't give a shit about anybody else being shafted, but when he realised that it was his brother, he started playing by different rules. The people he crossed are not the type to turn the other cheek. You upset these guys, and you end up like Jason and Mattie did. One dead, and the other crippled. Nobody messes with the people that run Croxley. That is until now. Some feathers have well and truly been ruffled, Mr Shannon and a lot of people like me are loving it. Let's enjoy it while we can, before the poor bastard doing the ruffling gets stamped on."

"So you think the Dark Angel will get stamped on, then."

"He is playing with some powerful people. It can't last too long before he's found out. It's as inevitable as Monday follows Sunday."

"Any ideas about who this Dark Angel is?"

Dillon raised his eyebrows and laughed. "Oh yeah, I'm going to tell somebody like you that. Whoever this Dark Angel is, he's a hero, and that's why nobody will say anything. We are sick to death of getting pushed around, and now, at last, we have got a voice."

"I noticed that you said he rather than she. Is that significant?"

"Go fuck yourself, Mr Shannon. You're the detective. And that hairstyle or rather lack of it don't do you no favours. It makes you look like one of the bad guys. Try growing it, and come up and see me sometime."

Now I know who said that. I always did fancy Mae West.

CHAPTER TWENTY-SIX

Charlie Keller is sitting on his balcony enjoying a breakfast of lightly toasted croissants and fresh ground Italian coffee. He looks down at the Mercedes in his driveway and the electronic gate that is slowly closing and waits for Frank Poole to appear. He hopes for his sake that he has some news on about the person killing his staff. The video shop was the last straw, and the sheep were getting even more scared. He needs to do something quickly to show everybody that he was still in command and that people can't mess with Charlie Keller and live to gloat. He flicks his cigarette butt over the balcony rail and throws the morning paper onto a chair. The headlines scream at him

DARK ANGEL STRIKES AGAIN IN CROXLEY VIDEO SHOP

He watches his security men busily walking around the grounds below him checking the security cameras and sensors. They know he is watching them so have intensified their work rate. They also know that he could have them killed on a whim, and Keller likes it that way. He feeds on people's fear of him, but he can feel it slipping away. He knows that there will be whispers that he is beginning to lose control, and he also knows that soon the sharks will be gathering to tear him to pieces if he isn't seen to be able to deal with somebody murdering his staff.

He is going to have to kill the Dark Angel himself, to send out a message. He will then cull his staff, to make sure that nobody gets any ideas above their station. He looks at his second in command Frank Pool, coming towards him. He has a smile on his face so hopefully it is good news. Unfortunately for Pool, he is going to have to be one of the first victims of the new regime after he has dealt with this killer. Keller feels no emotion abut planning the death of his second in command; it is how he has stayed in power for so long, by creating vacuums, so that nobody controlled the organisation fully, only him.

Keller doesn't offer Frank anything to drink or eat when he arrives on the balcony. He sits down and waits. He knows that there has to be news because otherwise Poole would not have dared come so early. "What have you got for me, Frank? I hope it is good news."

Pool doesn't attempt to sit down. "The killer finally made a mistake, yesterday in the video shop."

"Go on."

"When he came out of the shop, he didn't realise that we had one of the boys sitting in a car across the road."

"Who was it?"

"A Jamaican guy called Sparky. Nobody you'd know, boss.

"So where the fuck is he? Why didn't you bring him here? This happened yesterday, what took you so long, Frank?"

"The thing is, boss, Sparky got a little bit big for his boots. He saw this biker drive up to the shop and go in. When he saw him running out, he knew that there was something wrong, so he followed. He phoned me up around midnight last night and told me that he knew who it was that was doing the killing. He also said that he would only tell me if I paid him for the information."

Keller brought his fist down on the table. "So what did you do?"

"I arranged to meet him, said that I had the money, then strung the bastard up on a meat hook and beat the information out of him. He gave it to me, and I killed the bastard for his impudence.

Keller looked impressed. "And who is it?"

Frank Pool picked up the paper from the chair and sat down. "The killer has been right in front of our eyes from the beginning. Talk about not seeing the wood for the trees, boss."

CHAPTER TWENTY-SEVEN

DARK ANGEL STRIKES AGAIN IN CROXLEY VIDEO SHOP

By Thomas Brand

The Dark Angel struck again yesterday afternoon as Croxley was preparing for the weekend. The scene of the carnage, this time, was the Hollywood Video Shop in Pendle Road Croxley, where a lone motorcyclist attacked two men with acid and then inflicted serious injury with a blunt instrument.

A statement was read out by DCI Jenkins, who is head of the murder inquiry, which said that the police were following leads into the identity of the attacker and hope to be making an arrest very shortly. DCI Jenkins said that they wanted to speak to anybody who was in the Pendle Road area at around four o' clock yesterday. It is thought that the motorbike used was a black Honda or possibly Suzuki.

The men who were attacked are both in intensive care and are in an extremely poor condition though not dead.

I threw the paper down and finished off my bacon sandwich; I couldn't take any more. Tommy hadn't telephoned me yet, but I was expecting a call imminently. He had obviously pulled the information and tacked together a story from the police statement and some other sources that he had got. The fact that I had taken my phone off the hook last night because I was cheesed off with the world was probably the reason he had not got into contact. I had just put back the receiver ten minutes ago, though; he had by now more than likely given up trying.

I arrived back from my less than satisfactory meeting with Dillon Richard to find Shoddy in such a drunken mess that he was unable to open his door. I let myself in with a key that I keep in my flat for such emergencies. That fact that Shoddy was an alcoholic was brought home to me at times like these. I dropped a blanket over the armchair where he was sleeping. Kicked a few empty cans of cider around the room in an anger fit, and then let myself out and went to bed myself.

I had knocked his door at half past nine this morning, and then let myself into his flat. He was not there but had left a note apologising and saying that he had gone to the police station to talk with his mates and get some information. That was two hours ago, and I was kicking my heels wondering whether it was worth going into the office or going back to bed.

In the end, that choice was taken out of my hands by a sharp knock on my door. When I opened it, none other than DCI Jenkins was standing there, and he didn't look in the least bit happy.

He didn't wait to be asked to come in but pushed passed me.

"Come in, why don't you," I said, but my sarcasm as always was wasted on him. Jenkins just looked at life to literally for me to ever get through to the guy with any intellectual mind games. The only way I could really communicate with this guy would be to hit him, and I certainly wasn't going to do that. "Can I see your warrant, Mr Jenkins?" I said amiably.

"I don't need a warrant card, Shannon. I'm not arresting you, yet."

"So what can I do for you? Am I still helping you with your enquiries?"

"You seem to be popping up in this case with a certain amount of regularity, Shannon. First in Stanley Street, and now I find out that two men were killed in an alley at the side of your office. Have you got anything to say?"

"No."

"We could do this down the station if you don't cooperate fully. Where were you last Thursday at around 8 pm?"

"Now let me see; Mr Jenkins..........Mmm............ Oh yeah, now I remember, I was in the flat next door with my friend Shoddy. If I remember correctly, we were having a fish cake and chips supper and watching Dallas on the television. Shoddy and I love the Ewing family especially JR and Bobby. Do you like it, Mr Jenkins?"

"Don't give me that crap, Shannon. A man fitting your description was seen walking into that alley at around 8 pm. The bodies of those two men were found later, along with a lot of engine oil that must have come from a car. A car that was small enough to get down the alley in the first place. Have you still got that battered old Riley Elf, Shannon?"

"You know I have, Mr Jenkins; it's parked outside."

"Yes, and my men are looking at it now. Did you know that you've got an oil leak?"

"I probably have, but so do most of the other old bangers being driven around Croxley. Is there some special test that you can do to prove that the oil on the road in the alleyway came from a Riley Elf?"

"You were in that alley, Shannon; just admit it and tell me what happened. Maybe you didn't kill those two men, but if you saw something, I can book you for conspiracy to pervert the course of justice."

"I thought that was for somebody who actually said something that was a lie. I, on the other hand, am not saying anything because I wasn't there. Ask Shoddy. He will vouch that we were together all night."

"I'll tell you something now, Shannon. If we find any evidence that you were in that alley, I am going to throw the book at you, and I will tell you something else as well.........."

Unfortunately, I never had the pleasure of knowing what that something else was because a policeman appeared at the door who wanted a word. Jenkins went into the corridor, and whatever that word was seemed to send him into a frenzy. He disappeared down the corridor at lightning speed without as much as a goodbye. I looked over my balcony, just in time to see Jenkins running into his car and disappearing around the corner followed by two other police panda cars.

I didn't know what it was that caused him to rush off so quickly, but I suspected that it could be another murder at the very least.

There was nothing I could do but sit down and wait for Shoddy to come back. I made myself a cup of tea and switched on the television.

CHAPTER TWENTY-EIGHT

The Daimler DS420 glided down the A362 heading in the direction of Croxley. The car is one of the classiest limousines ever built and turns heads as it passes shops and houses. This particular model has been lovingly personalised with bullet proof windows and armour plating bolted on to the chassis. Inside the cabin, the seats have been reupholstered in black leather, with a drinks cabinet, tinted windows and a retractable window between the driver and passengers in the back, for extra privacy.

Keller and Frank Poole are gazing out at the bleak Croxley suburbs both locked into their own thoughts. It wasn't very often that Keller attended interrogation sessions that his men carried out, but this was personal. He was enjoying the thoughts going through his head about what he was going to do with the hammer he had in his coat pocket, to get to the truth about why his organisation had been attacked so brutally.

"So are we sure that your informant was telling the truth?"

"Sparky? I think that I can safely say, boss that he spoke the truth, as anybody in their right mind would do when they are bargaining for their lives. Besides, it all fits into place, although it will be nice trying to find out what the motive is?"

"You can't get to where I am, Frank, without making one or two enemies. It goes with the territory. I only hope that we get to know the truth."

"They all sing like little birds, in the end, boss."

"I'm not so sure about this one, but I hope you're right........what the fuck........"

Two police cars with their light flashing and sirens wailing overtook the Daimler. They turned into a road on the left and disappeared into the distance. Keller's driver put his indicator on, to turn left as well, and followed the police cars into the road. Keller slid back the glass screen.

"What's the address that you've got for our appointment, Bixby?"

"The address I was given Mr Keller is 21 Sycamore Terrace; it's this turning coming up on the right now."

"The big Daimler turned into Sycamore Terrace and immediately Keller could see that there were, at least, three police cars with their lights flashing, outside a house a few hundred yards in front of them. He hadn't seen what number it was, but he instinctively knew that it would be 21. His driver, Bixby confirmed that as they were approaching.

"What shall I do Mr Keller?"

"Drive on, as quickly as possible, but don't go over the speed limit just in case."

Bixby manoeuvred the Limo down several streets and finally got back onto the A362. "Where to now Mr Keller?"

"Stop here Bixby."

Keller turned to Frank Poole. "This is where you get out Frank. I'm going back home now, and I expect to see you there yourself very soon, with an explanation of what has happened."

Pool didn't say another word, knowing that if he did, it would quite possibly be his last. He opened the door of the car, got out, and watched as the tail-lights of the Daimler disappeared into the commuter traffic heading towards Bootle.

CHAPTER TWENTY-NINE

Shoddy didn't get back until mid-morning, and from the way that he was banging his fists on my door, I realised that he either had some important news, or he had been to the pub and was dying to use my toilet.

I let him in and as he walked passed me he slipped a piece of paper into my hand. On it, there was the hangman picture, only this time; the little figure had two arms and two hands. The letters underneath, however, were unchanged.

N _ T H _ _ _   P _ _ S _ N A _

"I need a drink, Moggs," said Shoddy, opening my fridge and pulling out two cans."

"There are no extra letters. What do we have to do? Guess the frigging words?"

"We don't need to do any of that, mate. Get your coat. We're going on a trip."

"Where are we going?"

"I'll explain in the car," he said draining the can and heading for the door. I grabbed my car keys and followed him.

"So what's been happening?" I said trying to keep up. Shoddy could certainly move when he wanted to.

We waited by the door of the lift, to take us down to the car park, and he went into his pocket and brought out a crumpled picture. "Recognise him?"

"It's Tommy. Where did you get it from?"

"I got this from police files, and it's not Tommy. His name is, or rather was, Leslaw Rusin."

"Well, he's the spitting image of Tommy. Who is the guy?"

The lift door opened, and we were hit by the pungent smell of piss and vomit. Somebody had spit all over the buttons; such was life in the flats. I averted my eyes as Shoddy pressed 'Ground Level.'

"This Leslaw Rusin character was a small time gangster at the time I was just a constable on the beat in Croxley. He wasn't particularly a bad villain, but sold dope and pimped for a couple of girls. We never bothered him much because as a sideline he did a bit of grassing for the police. I think that he may have grassed up the wrong fella, and he disappeared. Do you want to try and guess who the fella he grassed up was?"

"Oh, I don't know? Let me see............could it be Charlie Keller?"

"Bullseye, Moggs. I don't know the details because he was somebody else's grass, but he got paid for giving us some information about a post office raid in Bootle. This was 20 years ago, so back then; Keller was very much hands-on if you know what

I mean. He must have led the raid himself. Anyway, with the disappearance of Leslaw Rusin, so disappeared any chance of getting him into court. There is nothing like killing somebody to keep people's mouths clamped shut and that's what happened. Suffice to say not many people grassed on Keller or anybody in his crime network, after that."

The lift creaked to a halt, and we waited for what seemed like a good five minutes for the doors to open so we could make our way out, our lungs craving for proper air.

"Anyway, Moggsy, I got pestered by Rusin's wife, who knew that he had been killed by Keller, but without any hard evidence there was nothing any of us could do. She eventually left the area, but one thing that I do remember is that she had a son who was about ten at the time. This was around 1970, so that would make him......."

"The same age as Tommy is now," I said opening the door of the car. "So you think that Tommy is the son, who has come back for revenge."

"I can't prove anything, but I would put money on there being more to Tommy than he has told us."

"So where are we going now, Shod?"

"Just let's drive; I'll give you the directions on the way.

CHAPTER THIRTY

DCI Jenkins looks tense as they pull up to the multi-storey car park on Ridge Street in the unmarked white police van.

"Where the fuck is the bastard supposed to be, Harrison?"

"On the top level, sir."

Jenkins sighs. "So we had better get this street cordoned off and make our way to the top on foot. Have some of the lads go around the back, sergeant; you supervise, and the rest of you lot come with me." Jenkins begins the long walk up to the top level, and he orders the 12 men, carrying guns and wearing body armour, that are with him, to spread out as they reach the yellow and black barrier of the multi-storey.

A lot has happened since he had been given the information by his right-hand man, Sergeant Harrison, whilst he was interviewing yet another low-life. He had never liked Morris Shannon, but even in his wildest dreams, couldn't imagine that he could be involved in something as big as this. He just didn't have the bottle.

Jenkins isn't expecting great things from the information received, but it is always wise to follow up on any lead. The fact that the person who had made the call to the police station had known about the little hangman figure and is able to recite the letters underneath is the main reason why Jenkins has brought the 'cavalry' with him.

By the time he reaches the first level, even though it is cold and damp, he is sweating under his overcoat. He indicates to one of his men to take the stairs while he heads up the single yellow lines, used by the cars to go up and come down. There are a lot of vehicles parked on the first two levels, and his big worry is that it will be very easy for somebody to hide inside or behind one, and wait for him and his team to pass. He indicates to one of the marksmen with him, to stay on level one and make sure that nobody gets passed.

He wipes the sweat from his forehead; this is not there because of the exertion, but from the fact that he has been given so little time to prepare for this operation and is feeling very nervous. He could have done with twice or even three times as many men to shut down an area as big as a multi-storey car park. Christ! He doesn't even know who they are looking for. Is it a woman? Or is it a man dressed up as a woman as Sergeant Harrison suspects.

Jenkins and his men slowly walk up through level two and then three, leaving a man on each to guard any escape route. There are six levels in all, so three to go. On the top level there is a walkway that takes you to an entrance for the town hall; could this be the reason the murderer is here? Is somebody in the council one of the targets?

On the fifth floor, Jenkins's radio crackles into life, and Harrison's comes through. "Which floor are you on sir?"

Jenkins grabs the walkie-talkie. "Keep off this frequency, Harrison, unless you've got something important to tell me," he hisses into the mouthpiece.

Four members of the police team, start to walk up the ramp to the final level. They look nervous, and rightly so. He has seen what this monster can do and wouldn't want it done to him or one of his lads. He brings out a handgun, checks that it is loaded, and follows slowly behind. He tries to shrug it off, but he can feel his hand shaking ever so slightly as he approaches the top of the ramp.

CHAPTER THIRTY-ONE

It is 4 o'clock in the morning when the nondescript figure in the grey overcoat and balaclava arrives at the Ridge Street multi-storey car park. The wire mesh gate that bars his entrance makes him smile to himself at how easy a challenge it is to open. He pulls out some strange looking metal pins and gets to work. Thirty seconds later and he is pulling the gate closed behind him and walking up the stairs to level one, whistling tunelessly. Challenges like the gate were laughable, and he could have probably picked the lock with his car keys.

The car park is totally deserted at this time in the morning, which makes it the perfect place for his next little adventure. He throws a large brown bag onto the floor and gets to work. He starts off at level one, and by the time he arrives at level six; he is worn out after all of the exertion, and the bag is practically empty, apart from his tools. It is practically empty, but not totally, as he has one last job to do.

When he finishes, he leans against the car park wall and looks down at the street below. The top level doesn't have a roof, and he can see dark clouds overhead threatening rain. He looks at his watch. It's almost six o' clock, and everything is prepared. Later on today is showtime, and he has mixed feelings but understands that only a fool would be totally confident. People who are too confident make mistakes, and he can't allow a mistake to happen today otherwise, all of his hard work would mean nothing.

He had realised a couple of years ago that most of the people he would be dealing with were corrupt fools and idiots but should not be underestimated. Being a little bit scared had given him an edge, and this mixed with sheer hatred had made him invincible. It was at times like these that he wished, he could have shared his moment of triumph with the people that mattered to him, but they were all gone; long dead, but not forgotten.

By him anyway.

He picks up his bag, checks that all his tools are inside, and then makes his way back down to the first level. By 8 o'clock he is enjoying a full English breakfast waiting for the fun to begin.

CHAPTER THIRTY-TWO

The noise of an explosion makes Jenkins throw himself to the ground. His gun falls from his hand and bounces onto the pavement at the side of the roadway. He crawls over and retrieves it, cursing the situation he is in and wishing he hadn't put on one of his decent suits on. The sound has come from below their position, and he guesses that whatever has happened took place on the first level. He can smell burning and can hear the sound of car alarms going off behind him.

A voice comes through on his radio. "What's happening, sir? Is there anyone hurt?" It's Harrison, and he sounds frightened and confused.

Jenkins doesn't answer but looks around him and signals to his men to carry on moving up the ramp to the final level. He gets up, crouches down and walks slowly with his handgun pointing in front of him. He feels edgy. They are nearly up to the last level, and he knows that this is going to bring him and his men in full view of any would-be killer with an automatic weapon. They are going to be easy targets no matter what they do from now on.

"What's happening at your end Sergeant?" he whispers loudly.

"All clear here sir, but there has just been some sort of an explosion on the first level, and it's getting difficult to see because there is a lot of green smoke."

"Just keep watching sergeant. We are about to arrive at the top level."

"Will do, sir."

Jenkins is confident that he has done as much as he can to seal off the car park, considering his resources. As he moves forward and gets to the top, he is pleased that his hands have stopped shaking but fails to see the tripwire that he has just broken. It's only when several small sharp explosions go off all around him, and the air becomes engulfed in red and white acrid smelling smoke that he realises he has led his men into a trap.

Harrison's voice comes back on the radio. "There is a figure running out of the front of the car park, sir. What shall I do?"

"Can you intercept, sergeant?"

"It's difficult in all this smoke; I can't see a bloody thing."

There is another series of short, sharp explosions on the level just below, and Jenkins signals to his men to make a dash for the door leading to the stairs. As he approaches the door, the smoke gets thicker, and he prays that there is no sniper getting ready to put a bullet in his back. At first, he thinks that the door is locked, then realises that in his panic he is pulling rather than pushing it. When it opens, there is a delicious rush of fresh air mixed with the smell of urine and excrement that greets him. He and his men burst through into the corridor and begin running down towards the street below.

On the second level one of the squad snaps yet another trip wire, and inside the confined space of the stairs, the sound is deafening as the device goes off. The red smoke that now engulfs the five of them is impenetrable. Jenkins can feel himself beginning to panic and wants to vomit. He slows down to a walk and clutches the banister for support. When they reach the bottom and the fresh air, they are all gasping for breath and cursing whoever it was that set up the booby-traps.

Jenkins wastes no time. "Harrison? Where the Hell are you?"

"We are in pursuit of a blue Renault 16 registration number yankee, 667 charlie, hotel, romeo, heading on the A362 towards Croxley town centre."

"Stay with him, Sergeant, we are on our way."

CHAPTER THIRTY-THREE

As we make our way down the A362, Shoddy filled me in on his day.

"The police are still completely stumped by it all, but they have started linking the people that were killed, to Croxley low-life. Those two thugs that tried to beat you up worked for local gangs as did the two that died in the video shop. The two councillors and the police superintendent are the odd ones out, but it's common knowledge down the station that there is more to the Havana than just having a quiet drink."

"So you think that Tommy is on some sort of revenge trip because of his dad?"

"I don't know what I'm saying at the moment, mate, but it's an option worth looking at. You have to admit that there is a family resemblance. He has the motive...."

"Possibly."

"Ok, he has a possible motive, and the picture is the closest thing we have to a lead."

"Yeah, but hang on a minute, Shod. If it is Tommy that is doing the killing, then who is going to pay us for the work we have done? I just wrote him out a new bill; how is he going to pay it, if he is in prison?"

"Those are commendable sentiments, Moggsy. If Tommy turns out to be our murderer though and we bring him in, then think of the money you can earn from the newspapers for your story."

I hadn't thought of that. At the end of the day, we were in a win, win situation. If he was guilty I could get a big pay off, if he was innocent, I could collect my fee as normal. I sat back and relaxed, then noticed the police cars behind me catching up fast.

"Don't look now, Shod, but we've got a police escort."

"The leading car got close behind us, flashing its lights. I slowed down and started to pull over, and it shot past, with two others and a police van following behind."

"That looks interesting," said Shoddy. "I wonder where they are going?"

"Wherever it is they seem to be in a rush."

We carried on for another couple of miles, and then Shoddy pointed for me to turn right, down a road called Sycamore Terrace. I indicated and started to turn when a huge Daimler saloon shot around the corner, and nearly smashed into us. I shook my fist at the driver and the car stopped. The back door opened, and a man dressed in a suit got out and walked towards us. He didn't look very happy.

"No time for a bust up, now Moggsy. Calm your road rage down and drive on."

I stuck the car into first and completed my turn. "What number are we looking for?"

Shoddy looked at the bit of paper he had been navigating from. "It's number 21. That's the one over there on the right with the Renault 16 in the middle of the road and all of the police cars around it."

"Oh yeah, I can see it. Isn't that Tommy lying on the floor?"

Shoddy strained his eyes to see. "Do you know what, Moggs? I believe it is."

A policeman walked towards our car and put his hand up for us to stop. I smiled and waved at him, then reversed back. He didn't seem interested in following us and started to place bollards across the road.

"Great timing eh, Shod."

"Yeah, we seem to have a habit of being in the wrong place at the wrong time."

"What now, Shod?"

"I don't know about you, but I need a drink."

I turned left got back onto the A362 and headed for the nearest pub.

CHAPTER THIRTY-FOUR

Keller is sitting in his ornate lounge complete with wood-beamed ceiling and Georgian fireplace watching the BBC news reporter talking about the arrest of the Dark Angel. There are no up to date details yet, and the reporter is doing her best to make it sound exciting but failing badly. There is so little to say that they have resorted to old clips that have been shown time and time again about the murders.

The facts are very scant about who has been arrested, though there is some footage of the multi-storey car park from a distance, as it has now been cordoned off by the police, as has Sycamore Terrace.

The reporter is enthusiastic, but she's got nothing, and Keller eventually gets bored and switches her off. His face has aged ten years since the killings began and he has been getting tension headaches, which he puts down to a lack of sleep. He hopes that it is all over, so he can get on with the job of running his organisation. A purge is needed from the top down, and Frank Poole is number one on his list. He will be sorry to see him go, but he knows too much, and knowledge in this line of business makes people dangerous. As a reward for his hard work, he will make sure that it is done quickly so that he won't feel a thing. He is already mulling over who could be a possible replacement when the telephone rings. He picks it up and walks over to the balcony. In the garden, he can see two of his security men standing by the gate.

"Keller." He already knows who is calling as there very few people that have this number, and even fewer that would be brave enough to phone him.

"Boss, it's Frank. I've talked to a few of our contacts, and it has been confirmed that it's the reporter, Tommy Brand who has been arrested. They are holding him at Croxley Police Station. Apparently he was found with a load of implements used in the killings, so there's no doubt that this is our man. What do you want me to do?"

"I want you to kill him, Frank, and I want you to do it while he is in police custody. Is that clear?"

"Crystal clear, boss."

"Then I want you to come back here."

"Will do."

"Oh, and Frank.......................Make sure his death is as painful as possible."

Keller goes back into the lounge and pulls a Lugar Black Widow 9mm out of a drawer, checks that it is loaded, and puts it under a cushion at the side of one of the armchairs. He pours himself a Cognac, sits down and waits.

The fact that Poole has let this man be arrested is a mistake that he can't forgive. It sends out a message of weakness. By killing him while he is under arrest, it sends out a very different message. It shows that you can be got at no matter where you are, or who you are. This man needs to be crushed like an ant. He pays enough money out to the Croxley Police that it was about time he got some payback. Half of the CID were on his payroll; killing Brand should be child's play. He wonders how Poole is going to do it. Poison in the food? No, more than likely he will wait until he is getting transferred to a bigger station, like Liverpool, and do it then.

CHAPTER THIRTY-FIVE

"Mr Brand, I'd like you to take some more time to think about the statement that you gave us when we brought you in," said DCI Jenkins with a grim smile that didn't touch his eyes. He sat back in his chair, lit his pipe and waited.

Tommy Bland was unshaven and bleary-eyed after spending the last ten hours locked up in a cell underneath Croxley Police Station. Even though he looked the worse for wear, he still managed a smile, and when he spoke, it was with defiance and not as a man who was looking at a life sentence for murdering eleven people.

"I told you before, and I'm not going to change my story because it doesn't suit your preconceived ideas. I am not the Dark Angel, I had nothing to do with any of the killings, and I am not about to confess to something that I did not do."

"So tell me again, Mr Brand, just so I can get things clear in my head. What did you say you were doing in the multi-storey car park?"

"Like I told you, I got a call from somebody who said he had information about the murderer. He said that he wanted to sell me his story and claimed to know why the killings had been carried out. We arranged to meet in the car park."

"Funny place for a meeting, if you ask me," said Sergeant Harrison.

"Yes, Mr Brand, echoed DCI Jenkins. "It does seem rather a strange place to have a meeting."

"Look, gentlemen; I'm an investigative journalist. This is what I do. I put myself in danger so as to get a story that people can sit and read while they're eating their cornflakes in the morning. I'm freelance, so I have to work harder than your average reporter. Going to meet a serial killer in a car park doesn't seem all that strange in my line of work."

Jenkins shook his head and started to re-light his pipe. "So how come when we arrived, you were the only person in the car park? And, how come you had a bag full of some of the weapons used on the victims?"

"I told you. He got jumpy and saw you entering the bottom level. He set off some smoke bombs and disappeared before I had the chance to speak to him. I haven't got a clue how he did it, but when I saw that he had left his bag, I decided to take it and make a run for it."

"So what you are saying, is that you thought you were going to meet somebody with information about the Dark Angel, but when you got there, you realised it was him."

"That's correct. I had no idea before I set off to the car park that it was him waiting for me."

His description?"

"He was wearing a balaclava."

"So why are you so sure that it is a man?" said Harrison

"Because he sounded like a man, though if you insist, it could have been a very butch woman."

"If you were innocent; why did you run," continued Harrison with a practiced theatrical frown on his face, which he used when he was trying to convey disbelief to a suspect.

"Because it didn't look very good for me being found with a bag full of..........you know what? I don't even know what was in the bag because I never got a chance to look."

Jenkins pushed a sheet of paper across the desk. "Any of these items ring any bells?"

Tommy glanced down the list:

Sawn-off shotgun

Canister containing sulphuric acid

Axe

Various hand knives

A Colt combat handgun

Smith & Wesson .38 Bodyguard revolver

Pepper spray

Tomahawk (authentic Indian)

Unidentified liquid (thought to be curare)

"This means nothing to me," said Tommy pushing it back across the desk. Jenkins picks it up and studies it with a gloomy expression on his face. "So why did he leave his bag?"

"How the hell do I know? Maybe he was trying to frame me."

Harrison sighs. "It looks like he has done a pretty good job."

Jenkins puts the paper back into a beige folder and stares at Tommy with unblinking eyes. "Unfortunately, the bag was found in your possession, after a high-speed car chase. You were obviously trying to evade being arrested, which is not the action of an innocent man. These items on the list are all clean of fingerprints, which mean that as far as we are concerned, you've got them, so you own them. Wouldn't you say that's right, Sergeant Harrison?"

"I think that's a fairly accurate observation, sir."

"I've been writing about the murders since they started. Christ; I even coined the phrase that everybody is using, Dark Angel. This is what investigative journalists do, inspector; we fucking investigate. Besides, I have been asking around Croxley to see if I could get an interview, and my associate will be able to confirm this. I even sent him a message before I went to the car park, asking him to meet me there."

"Associate?" said Jenkins.

"Yeah; I hired him to ask around about the murders and paid him to get me an interview. In the end, all of those questions must have paid off because the murderer contacted me posing as an informer. The fact that I was at the meeting on my own is because I couldn't reach my associate."

"So does he have a name this mysterious associate of yours, or is he a figment of your imagination?" sneered Harrison.

"Oh, he's got a name alright. He's Croxley's only listed detective. Morris Shannon."

CHAPTER THIRTY-SIX

The last thing that you need when you have gone to bed after a load of beer and whisky is to be woken up by somebody banging on your front door. Shoddy and I had stopped off at the pub after our journey to Tommy's place and had spent the rest of the afternoon drinking and playing pool. Call it therapeutic, but it was a way of winding down after almost getting arrested. If we had been a couple of minutes earlier and had been knocking on his door when the police arrived, it could have been us lying on the floor keeping Tommy company.

We hadn't talked about the case much because there was very little to say. What needed to be said could wait until the next day, and after stopping for fish and chips on the way home, I said goodnight to Shoddy outside his door and made my way to bed.

It only seemed like a couple of minutes before the assault on my door dragged me out of semi-unconsciousness. In fact, it was 6 o'clock in the morning. It was only after getting out of bed that I realised that I had got in fully dressed and had not even bothered taking my shoes off. In hindsight, I should have put the chain on the door and checked who was on the other side was before opening it. As it was, I just flung the door open only to be pounced upon by a couple of uniformed branch police officers, who insisted on pinning me up against the wall. By the time I brought my eyes into focus, Sergeant Harrison was standing in front of me, shaking his head.

"Well, well, well, Shannon. What have we been doing this time?"

"I don't know, Harrison, what have we been doing?"

"I can think of several offences off the top of my head, but I think I am going to keep you in suspense until we get to the station. Cuff him, and bring him down to the car."

With that, he turned around and strode through the door.

Being handcuffed was a new one. Most of the times that I had been arrested, Jenkins usually didn't bother; this must mean that it was something pretty serious. When I got to the squad car waiting in the car park in front of the flats, Harrison was gone, which in all honesty was a bonus, because I hated the little weasel. I caught a glimpse of a blue Ford Cortina disappearing around the corner, before getting in the back between two policemen built like gorillas.

I didn't need to ask what this was all about. If Tommy had been arrested, it was obvious that as I was still working for him, Jenkins was going to put two and two together and come up with five. As we sped through Croxley towards the police station I wondered what exactly Tommy had told them about our working relationship. I had been in situations like this before, though never with the possibility of being charged as an accessory to 12 murders. I got the distinct impression that this was going to turn into a long day.

CHAPTER THIRTY-SEVEN

Keller hears the sound of the Mercedes on the gravel outside. He doesn't need to go to the balcony to know that it is Frank Poole returning because he isn't expecting anyone else. Besides, his security team would not have let anybody else in without consulting with him first. He doesn't bother getting up out of his armchair but checks his Lugar one more time to make sure that it's loaded.

Poole is taking his time coming up. He must be talking to the security guards. Maybe he is telling them that the service of only two would be required in future as the problem with the killer had been resolved. Having four guards on duty at all times was a precaution Keller had insisted on from the moment his associates at the Havana Club had been murdered. Even then, he realised that this was nothing but a direct attack on himself and that he needed some serious protection. The guards that he is using are the best in the business. All ex-SAS and trained to kill with either knives, guns or their bare hands.

He hears footsteps coming up the stairs and a little cough. Poole did that deliberately to make sure that his boss knew it was him. He enters the room and walks past the armchair, heading for the balcony. He doesn't see his boss sitting in the armchair, but when Keller says his name, he doesn't jump. He turns around calmly and waits for his boss to speak.

Keller doesn't waste words. "Brand?"

"He's dead, boss."

"How?"

"Well, unfortunately, it must have all got too much for him because he hanged himself in his cell using his shirt."

"Unfortunate indeed. Who did it?"

"I thought you would want me to do it personally, so I was left alone with him in the cell for five minutes."

"Did he struggle?"

"No more than most. Oh, and before he croaked it, I sent him your regards, boss."

"That's a nice gesture, Frank."

"Thanks."

Keller slides one of his hands under the cushion and grasps the gun. He is not going to reveal it to Poole just yet but shoot him quickly through the heart, so he doesn't feel a thing. That's the least he deserves for his faithful service. His men downstairs can dispose of the body in one of the usual places.

"You know, Frank, I was very disappointed that I never got a chance to speak to the Brand."

Poole nodded uneasily.

"Who do you think is to blame for that?"

Poole knows from experience after watching Keller kill men before that this is leading somewhere bad. He knows that he is only going to make it worse by trying to deflect the fault. "Me, boss; it's me who cocked the whole thing up. I should have gone for Brand as soon as I got the information about who he was."

"You know that I don't like failure don't you, Frank."

Pool nods his head and stares calmly when he sees the gun pointing at him.

"It's time for a change, Frank."

Poole nods his head. "Before you pull the trigger, boss, there is something that I have to give you. Can I?" He reaches into his coat pocket. "I took this off Brand before he died, and I think it will explain a lot."

"Whatever it is, bring it out with your thumb and forefinger, very slowly."

Poole does as he is told and brings out a small, black wooden box.

"What is it?" says Keller

"Before you shoot, maybe you should look inside."

"How about me shooting you, and then looking at what's in the box?"

"Because, boss, when you see what's inside, maybe you will decide not to shoot me."

Keller didn't look convinced but held his hand out. Pool passes him the box and presses it into his hand. Keller feels a small prick, and when he looks down, there is a small globule of blood on his palm. He wipes it on the armchair and flicks open the lid. The inside is empty.

"Is this some kind of joke, Frank?"

"No joke, boss." Frank walks slowly towards Keller and takes the gun from him. Keller tries to pull the trigger, but his finger won't move.

"Sorry, boss, but what I had to give you was not inside the box, but on the side of it."

Keller tries to lift the box up to see what is on the side, but can't.

"There is a little pin that has been dipped in Tubocurarine chloride. I obviously don't know from experience, but your whole body is probably feeling heavy right now and pretty soon you are going to find it difficult to breathe. Don't worry, though; this is not life threatening, and in a couple of hours the effects will wear off."

Keller tries to speak, but can't move his lips.

Pool disappears and comes back into the room carrying a large brown holdall. He stands in front of Keller, who is now finding it difficult to breathe properly.

"That little prick isn't enough to kill you, Mr Keller, but what I have got in the bag is."

CHAPTER THIRTY-EIGHT

"Hello, Morris, it's Tommy. If you are in, pick up will you, I've got something important to tell you........

Ok, you're obviously out. Can you meet me in the Ridge Street multi-storey car park at 12 o'clock today? I had a phone call that somebody has information about who our Dark Angel friend is. I need you as my bodyguard just in case it's a trick. There are a lot of crazy people out there."

The machine timed out, and Sergeant Harrison looked up and glared at me. We were sitting in one of the interview rooms in Croxley Police Station, and I had just listened to my office answer phone. The police had acquired it, and I was hoping that they hadn't trashed the place out of spite.

Sitting across from me was DCI Jenkins. He was in a blue shirt with huge sweat stains under both arms, with his top button unbuttoned and his red tie loosened to make him even more dishevelled that he usually looked. Jenkins gave the impression that he hadn't seen the inside of a bed for days, and from the body odour levels present in the room, both he and the Weasel Harrison were seriously challenged in the hygiene department.

Harrison came over to the table. "Shall I run the tape again, sir?"

"Did you hear that, Shannon? Can you identify who the person is on your answer phone or do you need a replay."

"It's frigging obvious who it is, Mr Jenkins. That is the voice of Tommy Brand, asking to meet me at the car park in Ridge Street."

"So would you like to tell me the relationship between you and Thomas Brand?"

"He is my client."

"And?" said Jenkins looking bored.

"And?.........I did a few jobs for him."

"What sort of jobs, Shannon?" Jenkins leaned over and gave me the eye treatment. I was determined not to look away, but in the end, he won. I suppose he's had more practice, and I was half asleep, and probably still a bit drunk.

"He had me following a bloke from the town council around and when those lads got blown away on Stanley Street, and he knew that I'd seen it; he hired me to get him more information."

"Did he ever ask you to try and get him an interview with the killer?"

"He did mention it, but I knew that there was not much chance of that. As you know, Mr Jenkins, if I had information like that I would have passed it on to the police."

Jenkins didn't look convinced "And that message? Do you have any idea who Brand could have been going to meet?"

I shook my head. "It could have been anyone, but if Tommy thought it would get him closer to finding out who the killer was, he would have met with the Devil himself," I added, "Am I under arrest?"

Jenkins sighed, got up and walked towards the door. "Not at the moment, Shannon, but don't book any holidays abroad for the immediate future."

CHAPTER THIRTY-NINE

"It's the law of the jungle, Charlie. You don't mind me calling you Charlie do you? No, of course, you don't, but as I was saying, it really is just the law of the jungle. Everybody is jumpy right now with this killer running around slicing people's heads off and generally being naughty. What is needed in the organisation is a new hand on the rudder; my hand, Charlie. Unfortunately, you are not going to be around to see how good I am going to be, but I have had a good teacher; you."

Poole is wearing rubber gloves, and as he talks, he is busy taking out two very long pieces of rope from his bag. Keller is barely breathing now, but his eyes are wide open, and Pool knows that he can hear what he is saying. He also knows that he is going to feel what he is about to do to him. He takes the end of the rope with the noose on it, towards Keller, puts it over his head and tightens it. He attaches the two pieces together, throws it over one of the wooden ceiling beams, walks over to the balcony and drops one end over the side. It hits the floor with a little to spare, as Poole knew that it would do. He has done his homework.

He walks back over to Keller. "I suppose you want an explanation about what has been going on over the past few weeks. I could tell you, but you really are an evil bastard, Charlie, and you don't deserve to go to your grave with any dignity. All that I will say is that you have been defeated by sheer hatred and blind ambition.

These are two emotions that are powerful on their own, but when moulded together, become invincible.

Poole checks that the noose is tight enough, and picks up his bag, which is now empty. "Goodbye, Charlie; may you rot in Hell."

Poole walks down the stairs and steps over the body of one of the security guards. There are two more bodies by the door and the fourth lying by the gate. He had bought a bottle of doctored champagne with him and shared it with the guards on his arrival to celebrate the death of the Dark Angel. He toasted the death with water having made an excuse that he was teetotal. There was so much cyanide in the alcohol that death was almost instantaneous. He laughed to himself how gullible people were. Fucking SAS of all people; trained to kill and survive the harshest conditions, but never considering that the person who had hired them was about to snuff out their miserable lives.

Poole gets into the big Daimler and backs it up until it is underneath the balcony. He gets out, attaches the rope to the tow bar, then gets back in and drives towards the electric gate. He can feel the tension in the rope and chuckles to himself as he stops and gets out again. He wonders if hanging from a noose has killed Keller or if he had already died due to asphyxiation caused by the drug. Before he closes the door of the Daimler, he drops a card on the driver seat. It is a picture of a hangman with a sad face. Below are two words.

NOTHING PERSONAL

He gets into his Mercedes opens the electric gates and drives into away.

CHAPTER FORTY

The news that the Dark Angel has struck again is everywhere. The fact that Tommy was in police custody when it happened had obviously put him in the clear, because he sounded offbeat and happy when he phoned me up, asking if I would collect him from Croxley Police Station.

The police had issued a statement in a crowded press conference that Thomas Brand would be released because the new murder of gangland boss Charles Keller, had put him in the clear. When pressed by a journalist from one of the major national newspapers, DCI Jenkins said that evidence left at the scene of the crime left no doubt that the murderer was the same one that had taken the lives of the previous eleven victims.

I could only assume that the conclusive evidence that Jenkins was referring to had something to do with the little hangman drawing. Only the killer would have known about this because even though I had told Tommy, he had not mentioned it in any of his articles.

When I went to Croxley police station to pick up my man, I was shocked at the camera crews and reporters waiting for him to come out. Tommy had all of a sudden become the centre of attention, and when he appeared at the door flanked by two burly policemen, I thought that he was going to be swamped. As it was, he fought his way over to where I was parked and jumped in. I had to drive through a mass of reports and cameramen that were trying their utmost to get us to stop and give an interview. I suspected that any interview that Tommy was going to give was going to be for a lot of money.

Finally, we were clear, but I didn't have a clue where he wanted to go. In the end, we decided that my office was as good a place as any, and I parked up in the alley at the side, and we made our way in. I checked to see if we had been followed by anyone from the press before I let Tommy get out of the car. Thankfully the coast was clear.

CHAPTER FORTY-ONE

Mattie sits in the kitchen of the small three bedroom flat that he is sharing with his cousin Glen. Ever since he and Erin arrived in Motherwell, they have been counting down the minutes and seconds to go back home. Here is out of harm's way, but it is another world, and they both feel like fish out of water.

Every time the phone rings, Mattie is hoping that it is the message that it is now safe for him to return to Croxley. But with each call his optimism has been gradually eroded until now, he feels that they are going to be stuck in Scotland forever. It's seven o' clock, and Erin has gone down to the fish and chip shop on the corner to get their supper. Glen is at work in the pub. Mattie has the television on but is not listening to it. He is staring aimlessly out the window and doesn't even realise that the phone is ringing until the sound of the key in the door snaps him back into reality.

He can hear Erin's talking. At first, he thinks that it is one of Glen's friends, but when she shouts, "It's for you, love." He springs into life and hobbles into the hallway, cursing his legs for not functioning properly. Erin hands him the phone, and takes the carrier bag with the food in it, into the kitchen.

"Hello?"

"Am I speaking to Mattie?"

"Yeah."

"Mattie, I can tell you now, that it is safe to come home. The problems that you have had have been resolved, and you shouldn't have anymore."

"So does this mean that you got all of the bastards?"

"Like I said, Mattie, the issue has been resolved. You won't be hearing from me again. So enjoy your life and get well soon."

"But hold on a minute........................"

The line goes dead.

Mattie walks as best as he can back into the kitchen, where Erin is dishing out the food. She looks up expectantly.

Mattie smiles, this is the first time he has felt hungry since he arrived in Scotland.

"Let's pack our cases, Erin; Keller has got what he deserved. The bastard is dead."

CHAPTER FORTY-TWO

"So are you going to tell me what this is all about, Tommy?"

"You're the detective, Moggsy. Haven't you worked it out yet?"

We were sitting in my office, and I had just given him a bill for my work plus expenses. I had made him a cup of tea to soften the blow. "I know that your father was Leslaw Rusin. I also know that Rusin was killed by Charlie Keller, and now, I know that Keller is dead."

"So all you have to do is join the dots, old son, and the mystery is solved."

"I'm too frigging tired to join the dots, Tommy; can't you make it easier for me and tell me what's going on?"

"What if nothing is going on? Or what if there is something going on, but I haven't got a clue either?"

"Oh, you not only know what is going on, Tommy, you are the instigator. I don't know how, but you are in this up to your neck, mate."

"So prove it, hotshot."

"That's just it Tommy; I can't prove anything. I wouldn't know where to start."

Tommy took a sip of the tea and winced. "Well, let's say for argument that I am going to write about all the events that have happened in the past couple of weeks."

"And are you?"

"As a matter of fact, Moggsy, damn right I am. The plot will be pure fiction of course, and it will be about a man who discovers that his father has been murdered by a ruthless gangland villain."

"Charlie Keller?"

Tommy laughed. "You wish. I told you, Moggsy, this is a work of fiction." He raised the cup to his lips again, decided against taking a sip, and put it put it back on my desk. He lit a cigarette instead and leaned back. "I'll tell you what. You tell me what you think happened, and I will give you some help in pointing you in the right direction."

"Well, for a start, Tommy, your father was killed by Keller. You are not going to deny that, are you?"

"No, I'm not. Carry on."

"You must have formulated a plan, so first you would have investigated what Keller was involved in and found out where he could be hurt. My guess is that you wanted to undermine his power and frighten him before you killed him. You obviously had help to do the killing, but I have no idea who. After that, mate, I am totally stumped."

"You're right so far. It was pretty easy to find out what Keller was involved in, and lots of people were happy to give me that information. The lives of scum like Mattie Webster had been destroyed by Keller, and they wanted him to pay. I had to obliterate the hold that he had over everyone by showing how vulnerable he was, and also get him to see his power slipping away.

"Before you killed him."

"Yeah, before I had him killed."

"So if you didn't do the murders, who did?"

Finding a person to do the killing was easy. In the course of my investigation I came across the perfect partner; a ruthless killer with plenty of ambition but not much imagination. I was going to blackmail him into helping me but in the end, I didn't need to. He was willing to help because he hated Keller too."

"So why make the murders so gruesome?"

"Use your imagination, Morris. At the end of the day, that's what the public want; blood, gore and cheesy headlines. They need a name like the Dark Angel to get through their dreary lives. The press is just as bad. They spend their time trying to find stories that will feed society's lust for the bizarre and sexually deranged. They're pathetic really. People are pathetic too. It's the herd mentality; the Nouveau Coliseum of the 1980s. If somebody else has died in a horrible way, they lap it up and read the details over and over. The

180

more horrific it is, the better Joe Public likes it. Do you think it's going to end here? This is going to be like the Jack the Ripper Murders; an unsolved gruesome crime that will touch the imagination of generations to come. There will be books written about it, theories in magazines, newspapers and endless documentaries. Every now and again some famous psychologist will say that he understands the deranged mind of the killer. What really happened? The Dark Angel was an idea that I had after a load of beer. The dressing up bit came from my partner. I guess he just liked putting on lady's clothes."

"I realise now that you got yourself arrested on purpose. But I can't think why."

"That's easy. With me arrested I become the focus of everything. My name is in the newspapers and on the television news channels. When I get released, the media people are like sharks in a killing frenzy. My story about how I met the Dark Angel is going to make me a fortune; I can name my price, and I tell you, Moggsy, it's going to be high."

"The hangman? What was that all about?

"I needed some piece of information that only the killer and the police knew. The hangman was perfect. It proved that I was not the killer. When Keller was killed, the little hangman figure was left at the scene, with all of the letters filled in.

"And me? Where did I fit into your plan?"

"You gave me my alibi. You could back up my story."

"So what's to stop me going to the police and grassing on you?"

"I don't think that you would do that. And if you did, I would simply say that you were involved as well. Even you must be able to see that if I go down, I can take you down with me." He got up from his chair, took a cheque from his top pocket and threw it on my desk. Plus, you would be a fool not to take the money and forget about what I have just told you."

I picked the cheque up. It was made out to me and was, at least, four times what I had asked for. Tommy opened the door. "Thanks for doing business, Moggsy."

"Hang on a minute. What were the two words written underneath the hangman?"

"Oh, those; just some nonsense I thought up when I was drunk. They don't signify anything, but I can guarantee that people will be analysing them till the cows come home for some hidden meaning. You can read what they are in my next column. Goodbye, Morris."

And with that, he was gone.

EPILOGUE

The man sitting on the balcony, in the Bermudan shorts and sunglasses, glances at the sky and jumps up spilling the contents of his drink over his t-shirt. Above his head is a helicopter, and being lowered from it on a winch is a man.

I didn't need to look too closely to know who it was. After all, I had been watching his programme for a couple of weeks now, and I had to admit it was addictive viewing.

"Mr Angelopoulos," shouted Tommy, over the noise of the engine. "Mr Angelopoulos, can you explain to me what connection you have with supplying Semtex bombs to IRA terror cells in Yorkshire and the Midlands?"

Mr Angelopoulos was joined on his balcony by two tough looking bodyguards wearing dark suits, but this didn't seem to deter Tommy "Mr Angelopoulos," he continued. "Are you aware that you are being filmed, and anything that you do or say is being recorded?"

The credits start to roll, with some frantic music in the background, and a hyped up voice informs us that, "Coming up in next week's episode of the Brand Report; an in-depth investigation on gun running in Britain." I switched off the television and Shoddy got up to make a cup of tea.

It hadn't been that long since my last meeting with Tommy and the fact that his cheque hadn't bounced meant that I wasn't desperate to find any more work. At the moment, I was being choosy and had already turned down a couple of divorce surveillances and a missing poodle. I was waiting for another big one, plus my girlfriend Cynthia had just got back from holiday and was taking up a lot of my spare time.

Things had gone back to normality very quickly in Croxley. The name at the top of the underworld may have changed, but nothing much had filtered through to the bottom. The drug dealers were still dealing, the protection rackets and prostitutes still provided illegal services for money and the council members were still as crooked as before. Apart from the victims, everyone seemed to have benefitted from the Dark Angel, but the person who had hit the jackpot was Tommy. With a book coming out that was sure to be a bestseller, a new investigative television programme that was top of the ratings and an influential column in one of the leading Sunday papers.

Who says that crime doesn't pay?

THE END

Thank you for reading the Penny detective. If you enjoyed it, pass it on and tell some of your friends. If you want to contact me with any comments, ideas or thoughts about the book, or just for a chat, look me up on Facebook: John Tallon Jones.

Email me at john151253@hotmail.co.uk to go on my mailing list for information about new books coming out. I never divulge any information to a third party.

I always reply and am always very happy to hear from you.

Other books in the Penny Detective series are:

1 The Penny Detective

2 The Italian Affair

3 An Evening with Max Climax

4 The Shoestring Effect

5 Chinese Whispers

6 Murder at Bewley Manor

7 Dead Man Walking

Before you go, here is a little bit of another book in the Penny Detective series.

Dead Man Walking

December 1986

CHAPTER ONE

I had just bought a shiny new nameplate for my office door; it read Morris Shannon Private Investigator in silver on a black gun-metal background. The plate was classy, and I had spent most of the morning staring at it, but the door itself was pretty grimy looking.

The door is at the end of what most normal people would describe as a derelict corridor. The dim 25 watt light bulb that dangled from the crumbling ceiling and the broken floorboards didn't do a lot for my business image, but this problem was mainly irrelevant due to the complete lack of clients.

The truth is that I work in a cramped rat infested space above a betting shop on Croxley High Street that probably hadn't even seen better days. Don't get me started on how shabby the High Street is either, or how that despite the drawbacks; this place feels like home. Maybe the town's looser mentality has rubbed off on me, or maybe I was born with it; for despite the fact that I was living and working in a shit-hole, I was feeling happy. I had my own home, a new girlfriend and now a shiny new nameplate. I was a proper private detective because that's what it said on my door. Think positive for long enough and the jobs would come. They always had done in the past, and who was I to doubt the future.

Outside my office in the real world, there was a clear, crisp winter morning heading towards lunchtime and dragging me with it. The weather was pretty commonplace on Merseyside for this time of the year, and I doubt if anybody took much notice of it. Christmas would be soon upon us again, and decorations had begun to appear in the most unlikely places. Even my business partner Shoddy had stuck some coloured lights up in his council flat and started drinking Snowballs with extra Cognac. The betting shop downstairs had an inflatable life-size Father Christmas that said yo-ho-ho if you pressed its tummy, and sometimes when you didn't. It was chained to the window to stop it going missing. The festive spirit was hard to come by around these parts, and inflatable Father Christmases weren't cheap.

I was just making yet another cup of tea with the same teabag, and debating with myself if it was too early for the pub when my thought pattern was broken by the telephone ringing. Now that was an unusual event! I looked at it long and hard, willing it to be a client, then jumped for it in a frenzy, before it had a chance to stop.

"Is that, Morris Shannon?"

Good question. "Yeah."

It was a man on the other end of the line, with a London accent.

"How can I help you?"

"Mr Shannon, my name is William Fitzpatrick, and I was wondering if your detective services included package delivery?"

"That depends."

"On What?"

"Is this something illegal that I'm going to risk getting picked up by the police, or is it something too big that I can't fit it into my car?"

He chuckled on the other end of the line. "A man with a sense of humour; I like that, but no, neither of those things. I need you to deliver something to my brother in Cheadle. It's nothing illegal, and it's about the size of a large book."

"Is it a book?"

"No, it's not a book, Mr Shannon................."

"Well? What is it?"

"Nothing sinister, Mr Shannon, but something that needs doing quickly and safely."

"So what about sending it through the postal service?"

"Impossible."

"Courier service?"

"The same."

This didn't sound right, and in hindsight I wished that I had listened to my initial instinct for danger, but I needed the money. Desperation puts a rose tint on any financial offer. "How come you need a private investigator to deliver this package?"

"Because I don't know where he lives. We haven't spoken for over ten years. The papers I want you to deliver are just documents he needs to sign so that he can access money from our father's will."

"So is your father dead?"

"Obviously."

"So why can't you take them yourself?" Christ, I was trying to talk myself out of a job, as usual.

"Because, Mr Shannon, I am phoning you from Aberdeen. It is snowing up here, and I just don't have the time to come to Manchester. I also don't have the skill to find out his new address. I am assuming here, that you do. Would my assumption be incorrect? Should I find somebody else, who has the required skills that I need?"

"No hold on a minute, don't hang up. I'm not saying that I can't do the job; I just want to know the details."

"Well the details are that I will send you the package this afternoon, and I hope that you are adroit enough to find out where my brother lives, at least by tomorrow. Is this possible?"

I was broke, and needed the money, so what the hell; it sounded like an easy job. "Yes, no problem, Mr Fitzpatrick, now about my rate per day................

CHAPTER TWO

"What do you mean; the cheque is in the post?"

I was sitting in my partner Shoddy's flat, which just happens to be next door to mine. Shoddy is a sceptical sort of guy, and who could blame him having spent the best part of his life as a police officer. Running around with villains and other policemen must do something to your head. In the end, you don't believe anybody.

"Look, Shod, I know that we always said money up front before we do any jobs, but this is different."

He slammed a large white bowl full of Irish stew on the table in front of me, sat down and began to eat his own. He crumbled bits of dried bread into the mixture and ladled in some sprouts. I shook my head when he offered me some; I draw the line when it comes to eating any food that is small and green

"A rule is a rule, mate. I thought we agreed after the last episode."

"Aw, common, Shod, how was I to know that the little old lady was a con merchant."

"Having someone offer to knit you a sweater for finding her lost poodle, doesn't constitute payment. It didn't even fit you for a start and what about my cut?"

"I told you we could share it, Shod."

"Yes, that's very generous of you, mate, but the fact is that it was my police pension that put these sprouts on the table, and those Christmas lights in the window."

Shoddy had a way about him to make you feel guilty. I wish I hadn't told him that Fitzpatrick was posting me the cheque, and because of Christmas, it would probably be delayed.

"So did you find out where his brother lives?"

He went into the pocket of his cardigan, pulled out a crumpled up piece of paper, and handed it to me. "That took me half the morning to find, and now you're telling me that I am not even going to get paid until after Christmas."

I opened up the paper. There was a name and address written on it

Barry Fitzpatrick

7 Springfield Gardens

Cheadle

"Thanks, Shod. I'm sure that cheque will be here tomorrow, or the day after at the latest. I'll get over to Cheadle as soon as I finish lunch and give him the parcel. I'll be back for opening time, and we can have a few beers."

"And what do you propose to use for money? We ran out of credit with Bill behind the bar, weeks ago."

"You'd better nip round to the supermarket and pick up some of that Bulgarian pear cider, Shoddy, so at least, we'll have something in to watch the TV."

He sighed. "That's like drinking diesel. Okay, Moggs, I'll pay for a couple of beers down the pub this time, but my pension isn't a bottomless pit. That cheque had better come through soon otherwise one of us is going to have to get a proper job. Now eat some sprouts; it's almost Christmas, and they'll get you into the spirit of things while I turn on the festive lights."

By two o'clock I was heading up the M62 in my Riley Elf, hoping that I would, at least, make it to Cheadle before it broke down. I wished that I had got a car with a bit more power under the bonnet. The Elf was a classic motor, but like Shoddy, it had seen better days and was in need of a good service.

By the time I reached number 7 Springfield Gardens, I was fighting against some seriously agonising cramp, which I always got on long journeys. The Elf was about the same size as a mini, and my six feet four-inch frame was probably more suited to something slightly bigger, like a Ford Escort, or even a Morris Marina.

The package really was about the size of a large book and was quite heavy considering that all that was inside were documents. I would have had a quick peek, but there was an official looking red wax seal, and lots of tape around the brown paper bag covering what felt like a shoe box. It had been delivered to the office about an hour after I had finished talking to William Fitzpatrick. The man who brought it was a nondescript looking delivery driver with a spotty face, dressed in a yellow jacket, with DHL Express written on the back. I assumed that all the money for delivery had been paid, so just signed a slip, took his receipt and didn't offer him anything.

I mused as I drove.............just how low would I go to earn some money? Sometimes I shocked even myself. My mum would have called it selling myself short, but I guess we all do that in some way or other. I tried to think of anyone that I knew that was totally 100 per cent happy, and after 20 minutes could only come up with my dad. It wasn't the fact that he was a multi-millionaire either. He was the sort of bloke that was just happy with what he had, and not worried about what he thought he should have. Maybe there was something of that in me though Shoddy always put my lack of drive down to no ambition, mixed with booze.

It's a fine line between having a happy or a sad life, and I seem to be crossing that line both ways rather a lot recently.

Finding number seven, which was where Barry Fitzpatrick lived, was not an easy task, mainly because most of the council houses didn't have any numbers. Springfield Gardens was seemingly devoid of a number seven, and I was beginning to despair, when I had a stroke of luck, and spotted a window cleaner. If anybody would know where the house was, then who better to trust than one of those.

He pointed me to a terraced council house near the end of the street with a garden full of car bits, which I had already passed a couple of times. I drove up and parked the Elf by some road works with the traffic lights on both sides permanently on red. The reason that I knew this interesting fact was because I had wasted about twenty minutes waiting for them to change, before an old lady, came out of her house and explained that they had been like that all day.

As I walked up the overgrown path of number seven, I noticed the curtains twitching in the houses either side; it was one of those types of estates. The majority of people who lived here were most likely on the dole and had nothing better to do. The way that I was dressed in a trilby and dark grey suit marked me out as either police or the man from the Prudential, both of which weren't welcome in streets like these.

Number seven didn't have any curtains. What served as something to block out prying eyes, was a blanket, which looked as if it had been nailed up over the window. Who lived in a house like this? I knocked and hoped that I was about to find out.

He was a tall man, with a forest of ginger hair growing out of his head and falling over his face before becoming entangled in a full ginger beard. A pair of tiny blue eyes pierced into my skull, which apart from an enormous red nose, was all that was left of his face, that wasn't hair.

"Who the feck is you?" He had a thick Glaswegian drawl.

I put on a brave face, smiled and held the package out. "Are you Barry Fitzpatrick?"

"I asked the question first, pal, and I repeat. Who the feck is you?"

He sounded like an abusive Billy Connelly; I didn't want to upset him. "My name is Morris Shannon, and I have here a package containing papers from your brother William. That is if in fact you are Barry Fitzpatrick."

"What is that gobshite doing sending me papers for. Do yehs mean newspapers?"

Oh God! Why couldn't even the simplest job I get, really be simple. I was in a dilemma. Should I tell him that his dad had died, or just give him the stuff and go? "Mr Fitzpatrick, I'm sorry to say.............."

"Fitz."

"What?"

"Call me Fitz; that's what everybody else does."

"Okay then, Fitz, I'm sorry to say............."

"Spit it out man; what is it that you are sorry about saying?"

"I'm sorry to say.................. That they are not newspapers, but apart from that I don't know anything; maybe you should ring your brother, and find out. I'm just delivering this package."

I held it out in front of me so that he could see.

He took it, turned it round in his large hands for a second, stepped back into the hall and slammed the door in my face.

Great; I wasn't expecting a tip or anything, but just a thanks and goodbye would have been nice. I made my way to the car, got in and started doing a three point turn to go back through the traffic lights. They were still on red, but nobody was coming the other way.

I was about half way through the roadworks when the explosion shook the street. It all happened so fast that it didn't register for a second. I felt the slight judder and heard a sharp crack like a load of fireworks going off. I stopped the car and got out. There was a gap where the door of number seven should have been, with smoke drifting around it. The window at the side had been blown out, and I was beginning to register in my nostrils, a terrible smell, like burnt pork. People were already running out into the street to see what had happened, and I had only seconds to make a decision about what I should do.

I jumped into the Elf revved her up and took off as fast as I could. I hoped that everybody would be too preoccupied with the explosion, to think about writing down my registration number.